The Redacted Sherlock Holmes

Orlando Pearson

Clink Street

London | New York

Published by Clink Street Publishing 2015

Copyright © 2015

First edition.

ISBN: 978-1-910782-89-7
E-Book: 978-1-910782-90-3

To my family

Table of Contents

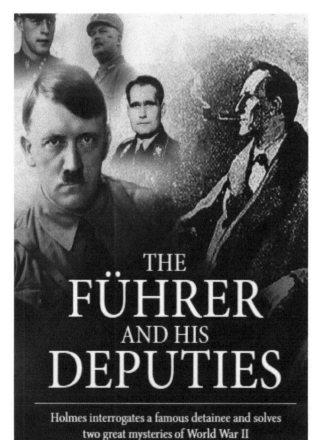

THE
FÜHRER
AND HIS
DEPUTIES

Holmes interrogates a famous detainee and solves
two great mysteries of World War II

The Führer and His Deputies

I have indicated several times in the past that there would be no further works about Sherlock Holmes. When I have done so, I have generally added the qualification that this was not for want of suitable material. After the Great War, however, relations between Holmes and me became much more distant as he retired to be an apiarist in Sussex. I had moved out of Baker Street after I remarried in 1907 and from then until well into the late nineteen-twenties I was busy raising my family with my second wife at our house in Queen's Square. Accordingly, while I continued to publish old cases occasionally, I had no recent ones on which to report. As time passed, these old stories increasingly wore the air of coming from a by-gone age. Thus, after 1927, I published no further cases at all as I had no desire for the work of my friend to appear as up to date as the penny-farthing bicycle or the mangle.

The narrative that follows recounts the only one of Holmes's cases from the second German war just ended in which I had an involvement. As might be expected, both Holmes and I were physically frail by the mid-nineteen-forties. Nevertheless, this case illustrates how my friend's extraordinary intellectual capacities were, with full justification, valued at the most senior levels across

Europe long after his withdrawal from active detective work.

In 1937 my wife died and, rather to my surprise, Holmes travelled up to London for her interment. At the wake we readily fell back into conversation.

"Come to Sussex, dear boy!" he urged. "My beekeeper's cottage could do with a bit more life. My housekeeper will remain in post with me, but she has saved enough to buy her own cottage in the village and will move there, which means that I have extra space. You will remember the housekeeper as Mrs Turner – the married name of Mrs Hudson's elder daughter – who ran the Baker Street flats with her mother after Mr Hudson's death. We can spend our time there defying the fading of the light. This time I will not even need to persuade a relative to buy your practice as your freedom from any smell of iodoform tells me that you have fully given up your work as a doctor in civil practice."

My children had by 1937 all long since left the family home and I found the idea of living in the country with Holmes far more appealing than living on my own in central London. It proved surprisingly easy to settle my affairs and within a month I had moved into Holmes's cottage.

There I planned to spend my final days and would have done so had the War not brought about a sudden change of plans. Our cliff-top village was an ideal location for a look-out and extended gun-battery to protect against the invasion feared in 1940. Our cottage was requisitioned and Holmes and I had to move out. With accommodation so short, I was concerned that we would not be able to find anywhere suitable to live, so I was pleased when, contrary to my fears, Holmes rapidly obtained the tenancy of a cottage near Fenny Stratford in Buckinghamshire. Thus it was that in July 1940 we found ourselves in the flat lands of the northern Home Counties, in a pleasant cottage with space for Holmes to continue his retirement activity of bee-keeping.

Fenny Stratford was such a peaceful village even in the Emergency that I expected few visitors. I was therefore surprised when a constant stream of people came to see Holmes. One such visitor routinely arrived on a bicycle with a gas mask covering his face. I could only catch the name "Alan" in the muffled speech which emanated from behind the mask when I opened the door. He always carried a large tea mug in his hand and, before coming into the house, he would detach his bicycle chain, which he then carried into our cottage over his shoulders on a rag to protect his clothes from the oil. Other callers – more normal in looks and behaviour – were also often on the doorstep. I had guessed that Holmes would have some involvement with the war effort, however tangential, and so in the atmosphere of secrecy which prevailed during the Emergency, I was not surprised that Holmes always asked for exclusive use of our small living room when visitors called. I either retired upstairs, or to our small kitchen. But, through the thin walls of the cottage, the odd word was audible, particularly when discussions became animated. If Alan was there, the voices were noticeably hushed and nothing could be overheard, but when anyone else visited, voices were frequently raised quite loudly. Sometimes, I sensed, quite considerable anger was vented. The German province of Thuringia – the province of Bach's birth – was mentioned with great animation, often in connection with bombs. I looked on the map and wondered why the focus of Bomber Command's air campaign should be the relatively small industrial towns of Jena and Erfurt, rather than the much bigger and more important Ruhr basin.

It was early May 1945 and the German war was all but at an end when a new visitor called on us. As usual, I vacated our living room, on this occasion retiring to the kitchen. I was just lighting a cigarette when Holmes put his head around the door and said "Watson, could I ask you to join us? Major Frank Foley has specifically asked that you be commissioned to make a record of this case."

My heart leapt at the suggestion and I joined Major Foley and Holmes in our sitting room.

"Mr Holmes, you will remember that in May 1941, Hitler's deputy, Rudolf Heβ unexpectedly landed in Scotland?"

Age had not withered my colleague's power of recall nor diminished the rigour of his spirit, so his response was a curt "Of course I remember it."

"I was the man who interrogated him. At the time there was general puzzlement that Heβ, a man so high up in Nazi circles, should have been so ignorant of German plans. He had flown to Britain and asked to speak to the Duke of Hamilton, but he did not claim political asylum, did not make any remotely credible attempt to present new peace proposals, and did not seem to have any worthwhile reason to have taken the great personal risk of flying here solo. He regularly claimed amnesia and then had patches where he remembered meeting people in the past. Since the announcement of the death of Hitler earlier this week, he has suddenly become lucid. He now talks at length about the Nazi inner circle and has made some startling claims about it which we are quite unable to disprove."

"Pray continue."

"At some point soon there will be a trial of the surviving Nazi leadership. One of Heβ's defences against being put on trial would be insanity. Our psychiatrists are divided as to whether Heβ is insane, while our Soviet allies have made it clear that they will regard any failure to put him on trial as a major breach of our alliance. We therefore want Heβ to be questioned by a man whose word carries weight both here and in Moscow and we want the questioning to be reported by a man of unimpeachable integrity – hence my request that Dr Watson joins us. There should be no doubt that the questioning has been thoroughly carried out and Heβ's responses accurately recorded."

Holmes shot a mischievous, side-long glance at me. "So, my dear Watson," he chortled. "After all my complaints that you embellish and romanticise my investigations, you are still regarded as an accurate chronicler of them. To pile a Pelion of additional irony onto an Ossa of existing irony, your recording of my complaints about the accuracy of the way you portray me is almost the only element of your stories that can truly be described as accurate." He turned to Foley. "And Heβ is still at Maindiff Hospital, in south Wales, I take it?"

"Yes sir. That is where it is planned that you should interview him as that is the easiest place to ensure both your security and his."

"And how do you propose to get us there?"

"Transport is at your disposal and will be here in half an hour."

Even though many years had passed since my soldiering days, I had remained organised and with few material needs, so in comfortably less than the time stated, I was ready to go, as was Holmes.

I shall not detain my reader with the tedium imposed by the exigencies of war-time travel other than to say that every effort was made to ensure that our journey was as swift and as comfortable as possible. It was a great pleasure, though mildly disconcerting, as dusk approached, to see house and street lights visible, cutting through the twilight, now that black-out restrictions had at long last been lifted.

It was late when we arrived at Maindiff. Quarters had been found for us in the Southern Lodge and we passed a quiet night. On the next morning, we had an appointment to see the psychiatrist Dr John Rawlings Rees, under whose care Heβ had been a patient.

"Heβ is frequently paranoid and suffers from hypochondria, but it is not clear to me that he can be declared insane," said Rees. "When he arrived, he talked about peace proposals and it was very logical that, as Hitler's deputy, he should have had access to them. But they were nothing different from what we heard directly from German sources ourselves – a largely free, though pro-German, western Europe, a free hand in eastern Europe and British overseas possessions untouched. The Germans had made numerous peace overtures along these lines since the start of the War."

"And we understand he has made suicide attempts?"

"Yes, in June 1941 and in February of this year."

"Did anything trigger these suicide attempts?"

"Heβ had no access to wireless or newspapers in June 1941, but he did in February of this year. This indicates a general mental sickness rather than specific external events tipping him over into suicide."

"What is his diet?"

"It is very ascetic. No meat, no alcohol. He is also a non-smoker."

"That would make him very similar to Hitler."

"You would have thought it might have been a way for Heβ to ingratiate himself with Hitler," opined Rees, "but that does not seem to be the case. Heβ has told us how he brought his own food to the various quarters that Hitler occupied even though Hitler had a vegetarian cook at his disposal for his own use, so preparing vegetarian food for Heβ would not have posed a problem. This behaviour disconcerted Hitler so much that Heβ used to eat separately from him. He has been very hard to feed here and has had to be threatened with force-feeding. This attitude towards food may, of course, be part of his paranoia."

"And how does Heβ fill his days?"

"He is well-treated. Those were the instructions from the most senior level. He spends most of the time in bed, though we have taken him out for drives into the Monmouthshire countryside, and he goes for walks around the grounds of this hospital – although, as you will understand, he is at all times under guard."

"And what does he do for mental stimulus?"

"He can write letters to his family and he keeps a diary. He also has use of the library."

"What does he read?"

Dr Reese paused, and his gaze flickered between Holmes and me before he answered.

"Well, Mr Holmes," he said eventually. "We encourage him to read the works of Dr Watson here. Heβ has an excellent command of English as that was the language of business in Egypt where he was brought up. Accordingly, he can read whatever he likes, but we find detective fiction is great comfort literature for someone in his volatile state and that is why we encourage him to read Dr Watson's works. Something excessively exhilarating may make a sane person mad, but Dr Watson's works are an excellent way of keeping an overwrought man sane as they are both stimulating and normally have a logical outcome."

There was a pause before Holmes gave a rather bitter laugh. "Almost the first thing I said to you, Watson, before we moved into Baker Street was that I get in the dumps at times, and may not open my mouth for days on end. I need to be left alone then, I told you, and I soon get right. You could hardly state a clearer description of the symptoms of someone who is on the edge and yet Herr Heβ is given your books about me to ward off hypochondria, paranoia and suicidal tendencies. I note that although everything else in this country is tightly rationed, irony is here in plentiful supply."

"And his amnesia?" I asked.

"It fades in and out. Sometimes he claims to remember nothing even when we show him pictures of himself and his associates in his pomp. But he writes letters which show an understanding of both his past and of the present."

Our initial interview with Heβ was set for two o'clock that afternoon. We met him in a comfortable room with three old but imposing armchairs, arranged so that Holmes and I were facing Heβ. We took our places and Heβ was brought in by a medical orderly. He had deep-sunk, suspicious-looking eyes and was extremely gaunt. He wore a shirt without a tie and a lounge suit, but such was his thinness that the jacket extended down much further than would normally be the case.

Heβ sat down and the orderly left us. Holmes adopted the practised, airy manner he took when he wanted to make an interrogated party feel at ease. "I am Mr Sherlock Holmes, and this is my colleague Dr Watson, who is to make a record of our discussions and before whom you can talk as freely as you would with me. We want to establish your state of mind as this great European conflagration comes to its close. So Herr Heβ—"

"What are you doing here?" Heβ interjected. "Are you trying to poison me as well? Look at this food they give me!" He wrenched a rather fluff-flecked sandwich out of his pocket. "I am sure it is poisoned. Would you care to try it? Do you have any food I can swap with you?"

"Herr Heβ, I am here to talk—"

"Herr Heβ, Herr Heβ ... It is not so long ago that you would have had to address me as Herr Deputy Führer and if I had not broken off my studies at the University of Munich to pursue my political ambitions, I would at least have the title of Herr Dr Heβ. It is only four years ago that I deputised for the Führer at the Mayday celebrations. *Sic transit gloria mundi.*" He fixed us with a wild-eyed stare. "After I flew to Scotland, the Führer stripped me of my titles and ordered that I be shot on sight if I return to Germany, so you may as well, I suppose, call me Herr Heβ." He paused and turned his face to the window though I noted his eyes were straining to look at Holmes from side-on. "And you are the famous Sherlock Holmes?" he asked. And then "Are you sure the Führer is dead?"

"His death was announced on Hamburg radio on 2 May," Holmes confirmed calmly. "He is believed to have committed suicide, although the announcement talked of him dying on the front-line, fighting against Bolshevism. The Soviets have taken Berlin and the end of the War can only be days or hours away."

"Has his body yet been discovered and identified?"

"The battle for Berlin has barely concluded. Recovery and identification of his body are hardly going to be the most pressing requirements," said Holmes.

"If he is dead, you will not find his body," said Heβ, his deep-set eyes now staring out into the room. "Or if you do find a body that someone claims is his, it will be so damaged as not to be identifiable." He suddenly turned to me. "We have much in common, good doctor!" he exclaimed. "We both act as amanuenses, writing down the words and moulding them for people who become much better-known than ourselves."

I had not expected to do much more than record what

Holmes and Heβ said, so I was somewhat taken aback by this remark.

"Yes," continued Heβ to me. "When Hitler and I were prisoners together in the Landsberg prison after the Bierhallputsch, he dictated to me the work that became known as *Mein Kampf* or *My Struggle*. He wanted to call it *Four and a Half Years (of Struggle) Against Falsehood, Stupidity and Cowardice*. The brackets are particularly fine, I think. I am sure that if your friend had had his way, your novel *A Study in Scarlet* would have been called *A Monograph on the Apprehension of Drivers of Vehicles for Hire (with observations on the analysis of blood stains in dust)*. Note those brackets again."

Holmes opened his mouth to say something though whether to express his preference for Heβ's suggestion or to deny what he was saying, I could not be sure. But before he could say anything, Heβ ploughed on.

"Yet your friend gets all the fame, Dr Watson, just as Hitler gets all the plaudits – and all the royalties – for *Mein Kampf*."

Holmes and I had agreed a signal if we wanted a break in the interrogation – if we felt physically threatened by a man forty years younger than ourselves, or if Holmes wanted to consult with Major Foley about the progress of our discussions. Knowing Holmes and his well-justified confidence in his own methods, I had thought we were most unlikely to see the need for anything of the sort. As events unfolded, it was, in retrospect, a mistake to use phrases inspired by Holmes's simulated ravings in "The Dying Detective" as a basis for our code, but Holmes suddenly turned to me and said "I think we need to consult with Mr Culverton Smith."

We retired to the corridor outside the interrogation room to consult. Because there were numerous security and hospital staff there, Holmes took me to one side so that we could talk alone. "As a doctor, do you have an opinion on whether there is any point in continuing this interrogation?" he asked.

"Heβ certainly exhibits paranoia about his treatment, but he also has command of facts. He knows who we are and recalls some of the events of our collaboration. He has made a startling prediction about the body of Hitler, which we cannot at this stage disprove. He is clearly able to defend himself. If I may make so bold, Holmes, he seems to be asking you more questions than you are asking him. Perhaps we should ask him why he came to Britain."

We went back into the room and found that Heβ had adopted a crouched position beside his armchair. He was whistling tunelessly between his teeth. When he saw us, he straightened himself up and sat back in his chair, though his eyes continued to roll.

"So, Herr Heβ, what brought you to Britain?"

"Why do people fly to another country?" asked Heβ airily and paused before continuing. "They may have a commission to perform ... They may have people they want to see ... They may be going on holiday ... They may be trying to escape from something." Heβ stared at us as he stated the different possibilities as though he was trying to gauge our reaction to each.

"And which of these applies to you?"

"I did not come here on holiday. Ever since the British expropriated my family's business in Egypt after the Great War, I vowed to have as little to do with them as possible. I only came here because I had no choice."

"And why did you have no choice?"

"Oh, Mr Holmes, you can surely do better than that! Your friend leads us to believe that you are one of the great minds of Europe! Is Mychett Place in Surrey, where

I was detained for a while soon after I arrived here, not close to where William of Ockham, the man with the famous razor, was born? Why are you so slow in applying that blade of his?" Heβ drew his hand slowly down his face in the gesture of one using a safety razor, and then suddenly pulled his hand in a slashing motion across his throat. "Has your chronicler here not quoted you as saying that once you exclude the impossible, whatever remains, however improbable, must be the truth. So exclude, my dear Mr Holmes, exclude."

Holmes turned to me. "Did you have me say that?"

"On several occasions. And you said it on several occasions."

"Have you any change in your pocket?" piped up Heβ almost before I could finish my sentence.

"Yes," said Holmes.

"Any silver?"

"A good deal."

"How many half-crowns?"

"I have five."

"Ah, too few! Too few! How very unfortunate, Mr Holmes! However, such as they are, you can put them in your watch pocket. And all the rest of your money in your left trouser pocket. Thank you. It will balance you so much better like that."

I do not think I have ever seen my friend so nonplussed. I noticed him momentarily consider doing as Heβ had bid, although he quickly thought better of it. Our other code for leaving the room had been to talk about the prolixity of oysters, but as Heβ's non sequitur about the distribution of small change was itself a direct quote from "The Dying Detective", I was reluctant to resort to it. I was unsurprised when Holmes rose without saying anything and made for the door again. I followed him.

"The case gathers in interest," said Holmes calmly, although after he had said this he drew deeply on the cigarette he had lit immediately after we had left the interrogation room, so that its tip burned a fierce red. I was reassured by this response. If Holmes could see our problem as an intellectual challenge, then I was sure that he would bring it to a satisfactory conclusion. If he merely regarded Heβ as a madman, we were unlikely to progress. "Let us play his game. He has given us four reasons why he might have come to this country. One we have eliminated. Perhaps we should talk to Major Foley about what specific peace proposals or insight into German plans Heβ brought when he arrived here four years ago. That would reflect a commission to be performed."

Foley was called.

"There were no proper peace proposals, Mr Holmes," he said. "Hitler repeatedly made peace overtures in the early years of the War, but Heβ came with nothing new. And we had already warned Stalin that Hitler was about to attack him. But if he believed us, he took no action. Heβ told us nothing we did not know already even though his landing was only seven weeks before the Germans attacked the Soviets."

"Very well," said Holmes. "So he was not performing a commission and he was not here for a holiday." I saw Foley start at the latter suggestion, but before he could respond, Holmes had spun around and, showing a surprising turn of speed, he went back into the room. I followed at a slightly slower pace.

"So why did you want to see the Duke of Hamilton?" asked Holmes.

"I understood that as a Duke he could tell Churchill to make peace."

"Had you met the Duke of Hamilton previously?"

"I had seen him at a function in Berlin during the Olympics in 1936, but I had never spoken to him."

"So why did you think he could tell Churchill to make peace. Neither in Germany nor in Britain can a duke tell a political leader what to do just because he is a duke."

Heβ was silent.

"What were you afraid of, Herr Heβ?"

There was a long pause. When at last he spoke, Heβ's voice was hushed to a conspiratorial whisper: "Have you heard," and his eyes grew wide as he posed the question, "of the Wuwas?"

I could see from Holmes's face that he had not.

"The Wuwas?"

"Yes, the Wunderwaffen." Heβ nestled back in his chair and smiled as he saw the look of puzzlement on Holmes's face. "Miracle weapons. I hear how they rain down on London. When in 1941 the British did not listen to me about Germany's imminent invasion of the Soviet Union, I assumed that they would make common cause with the Germans against the Soviets and that I would be sent back to Germany. That was why I attempted suicide in June 1941. And my fear of the success of the miracle weapons was the reason why I attempted suicide in February of this year."

"So you feared a German victory when you came here?"

"Have you heard of Ernst Röhm?"

"Head of the Storm-troopers, arrested and murdered in 1934."

"Actually the chief of staff of the Storm-troopers. Hitler was its supreme leader, or Oberster Führer. Executed in 1934."

"Are these distinctions important, Herr Heβ?"

"Do you know how Röhm was arrested and killed?"

"Herr Heβ, it is normally the interrogator who asks the questions."

"Did you know that Hitler personally arrested Röhm? He arrived at a hotel where Röhm was staying and shouted 'Röhm, du bist verhaftet', or 'Röhm, you are under arrest.' Note the 'Du'. Röhm was one of the very few people to whom Hitler said Du – the familiar form of your word 'you'. Röhm and Hitler used it to each other because they had known each other right from the very beginning of the National Socialist movement. And Hitler said it while he was arresting Röhm and arranging for his death."

"Why are you telling us this?"

"Have you not thought how strange it was for the Führer to make the personal arrest of one of the very few people he was on familiar terms with?"

Holmes was silent.

"He must have had a very strong reason for doing this. Would your Mr Churchill personally arrest Mr Atlee, and would he address him as Clem as he did so?"

"So what is your explanation?" asked Holmes, clearly puzzled by the direction of the conversation.

"Have you heard of Eva Braun?"

I could see from Holmes's face that he had not, just as her name was entirely new to me.

"She is – or was – Hitler's mistress," said Heβ.

Holmes looked stunned, a feeling I shared. The name and even the idea that Hitler might have had a mistress were completely unknown to us. Heβ must have been able to see the effect he had had. With a beaming smile, he pressed home his advantage.

"Ah, there's the genius and the wonder of the thing!" he exulted. "She goes everywhere Hitler goes, is well-known in the top circles of the NSDAP, and no one has heard of her. That is what puts German news organisations on a pinnacle for preserving secrecy."

"You make her sound like my old adversary, Professor Moriarty."

"Fräulein Braun would never have made it to being a professor. She is or was an intellectual vacuum. Hitler met her when she was a photographer's assistant. She is attractive to look at, knows something about photography and film-making – and that is the limit of her intellectual prowess. When history comes to examine her, it will find her a vapid disappointment. Röhm became her lover as well as Hitler. When Hitler found out about it, he insisted on arresting Röhm personally so as to minimise the chances of word about the various relationships coming out."

"But when Röhm was arrested, all the press carried stories of his homosexuality. What makes you say that Röhm and this Eva Braun woman were lovers?"

"Don't you say, Mr Holmes, that the press is a useful tool if you know how to use it? Our RMVP knows how to use the press."

"RMVP?"

"Reichsministerium für Volksaufklärung und Propaganda, the Imperial Ministry for the Enlightenment of the People and for Propaganda. Led by Dr Josef Göbbels. The stories about Röhm's preferences were from the German press agency, which is fully under party control. The *Völkischer Beobachter*, *The People's Observer*, is not quite the same as your *Observer*, even though Germans edit both. People in Germany do not buy newspapers in order to turn to the back page to find out what is going on in the world of sport, or to the centre pages to read society tittle-tattle. They buy newspapers to find out what the government wants them to think. And then they do so.

Our *Observer* will report as it is instructed by the government. It was not even necessary to have Röhm shot, to spread word of his supposed preferences, although doing so made the chances of anyone wanting to investigate it and exposing it as a lie much more remote."

"So what does the fate of Ernst Röhm have to do with you?"

"After Röhm had died, Eva Braun and I became lovers. When I visited the Führer's headquarters, I used to eat separately from the rest of Hitler's inner circle. Eva would make an excuse to join me. Sometimes our meal got extended." Heβ's face broke into a lop-sided leer at the memory.

"So you left Germany because you were afraid your relationship with Eva Braun had been discovered?"

"Ah, Herr Holmes, you have eliminated the impossible and arrived at the however-improbable truth! I congratulate you!" Heβ stared out and went through a fit of blinking. "After what happened to Röhm, I did not want to take the risk of the relationship between Eva Braun and me being found out."

"Why did you think your relationship with Eva Braun might have come to the attention of Hitler?"

"Hitler had a new bodyguard called Otto Günsche. He was a tall good-looking man, much closer in age to Braun than I. Eva had switched her affections to him. I had sidelined Röhm by tipping off Hitler about the relationship between Röhm and Fräulein Braun. Röhm died. Günsche had surprised the secret of Eva Braun and me, so I thought the same thing would happen to me. Britain was the only place I could fly to. At the time, Germany had neutralised all its enemies apart from Britain. All the non-belligerent countries would have sent me back. Only Britain would regard me as a trophy worth retaining."

"Did Hitler not punish Braun for her infidelity?"

"My dear Mr Holmes! We Germans are a civilised race when it comes to how we treat ladies. We do not mobilise them like you do and put them to work in arms factories. We do not halt the production of their cosmetic products for the war effort. We allow those in domestic service to stay in domestic service. And we do not punish them for their side jumps." And here Heβ stood up, pulled up the bottom of his over-long jacket as though he were a woman raising her skirts, pranced first one way, then the other, and sat down again.

"Side-jumps?" asked Holmes calmly.

"We do not punish them for their ..." Heβ paused for a second as he sought the right English word, "... indiscretions. We leave that to the English and their Henry VIII."

"What can you tell us about Eva Braun and Hitler?"

"They became lovers in the early thirties. Hitler was not a very ardent or attentive lover and so Eva sought solace in the arms of others. After Röhm, it was I. It was easy to make the excuse that the Führer wanted me so I could disappear from Ilse, my wife. And with the Führer constantly travelling around, it was easy for me to have time with Eva Braun. She was always whisked out of the room whenever anything of substance was discussed and, since I and the other leading figures in the senior circle of ministers and advisers had overlapping responsibilities, it was easy for me to slip out too. I expect that Günsche shot the Führer when his liaison with Braun was discovered in the last days of the battle for Berlin, as he wanted to protect himself from the same fate that had met Röhm, and the fate which would have met me had I stayed in Germany. And Günsche will make sure the body is destroyed. The Germans will want to know that their leader died a hero's death and will not want any examination of the powder marks on Hitler's body to show that the fatal shot was fired from a German standard issue at a distance greater than at arm's length. That would suggest it was the result of some vulgar matter of the heart rather than a hero seeking the free death."

"The free death?"

"Committing suicide rather than falling into the hands of the Bolsheviks."

"You make yourself very clear."

"Now you know the truth, can I have some unpoisoned food? What they give me causes me to become irrational." He slumped back in his chair, stared up at the ceiling and started whistling.

At a nod from Holmes, we retreated to the corridor.

"Do you believe him?" I asked Holmes.

"I am sure," said Holmes, "that Heβ can defend himself if he wants to, against any charges. We must remember that as much as establishing guilt, the forthcoming trial will be about finding out what happened and why, and that will be easier to do if Heβ is there. He is intermittently lucid and when he is not lucid, he does not talk about matters of substance. Once the final terms of any surrender are worked out, and the Allies are in full control of Germany, there will be no reason not to send him back. We should find out his reaction to the prospect of that."

We went back into the room.

"Herr Heβ," said Holmes. "You do realise that you are almost certainly to be indicted as a war-criminal and tried in Germany? You are likely to be charged with war crimes and crimes against humanity."

"From 1933 to September 1939," replied Heβ in a voice of the utmost serenity, "there was no war and I was the legally appointed deputy leader of a sovereign nation at peace. Accordingly, no charges can arise. From May 1941 until now, I have been a prisoner. Between September 1939 and May 1941 I had only a modest role in the workings of my nation's government. Everything was decided by Hitler, whose company – for reasons you will now perhaps understand – I took pains to avoid. Therefore, I was not there when the major decisions were made. A Deputy Führer is still a deputy and my role, insofar as I had one, was largely confined to agreeing with what the Führer said. As there is apparently now no danger of being shot on sight if I return to Germany, I can face going back with equanimity."

This was spoken with Heβ looking unwaveringly straight at us. It was as if the outlandish version of Heβ that we had intermittently seen during our prolonged interview was a persona that had never existed.

We went to consult with Foley again.

Holmes spoke first. "Heβ has lurched from implausible raving to calm rationality with every shade in between. Much of what he has said is completely new to me and I am unclear what it tells us about his state of mind or about the state of affairs in Germany."

Foley said "We have had no way of substantiating the more outrageous things he has said to us. We know so little about what is happening in Germany other than that there is chaos."

Holmes smiled and said "I have my methods and I propose to apply them to see what I can substantiate. We will report back to you in a week."

Holmes and I were brought back to Fenny Stratford and I could see that Holmes had a plan for what to do next, but he seemed reluctant to tell me.

After we had been back for a day, he finally spoke. "It is

a very major responsibility I take onto myself, but I suppose I can let you into the secret of my war work as you have been given carte blanche to write a full and honest account of this case. The visitors you have seen come to our cottage – Alan, who wears the gas-mask, and the others, who are colleagues of his – are amongst the greatest minds in the country. They are based at the great house in Bletchley Park and have been engaged in breaking German military codes. Alan has been leading the team that has done this and occasionally has asked me for help on difficult details of the coding structure. My trifling monograph on codes, in which I analyse one hundred and sixty separate ciphers, was apparently a great source of inspiration to them. When they decrypt a German military message, they enter any personal details of anyone they find out about onto a card file, so that files on millions of German personnel are kept. I wonder if we could get Alan to check into the existence of Otto Günsche and Eva Braun for us?"

Alan called the next day, wearing his gas-mask as usual and displaying all the other eccentricities to which I have already alluded. I was asked to join him and Holmes in our tiny sitting room. I noted that Alan used the bicycle chain he brought into the house to secure his tea mug to a radiator. Holmes asked him to see what he could find out about Otto Günsche and Eva Braun, though I noted he gave Alan no indication of why he wanted the information. The voice that assented to Holmes's request was somewhat muffled behind the mask, but I was not surprised when, a few days later, Alan returned with an envelope in his hand.

For his second visit, Alan retained the gasmask over his eyes, but now he turned it upside down, leaving his mouth and nose clear so that the breathing apparatus stuck into the air like the spout on a teapot. Accordingly, his voice was much easier to understand.

"We know Günsche as a Sturmbannführer or major in the Leibstandarte," he began. "That is to say, the personal bodyguard of Adolf Hitler. He started in the role in 1940, had prolonged periods at the front in 1941 to 1943, but has been Hitler's personal adjutant since March 1944. We know nothing about any Eva Braun. We have no record of anyone under that name, but all our focus has been on military personnel and so we have very few records of women in our indexes."

When Alan had gone, Holmes filled the bowl of his pipe and smoked in one sitting until it was empty.

At length he said "It is striking how much of what Heβ has told us is plausible. We know about the death of Röhm, though he has allocated a different cause to it than what was reported in the controlled press. We now know that Otto Günsche is a real person who is in Hitler's personal bodyguard. We also know that any explanation for Heβ's flight other than fear has been explored and found wanting. Furthermore, when a return to Germany for a potentially capital trial was put to him, he provided a rational argument for his defence. My inclination accordingly is to state that he is sane to stand trial, but he seems to be too harmless to face a capital punishment."

"What about the other claims he made: that no body will be found, and of the relationships between Hitler, Heβ, Röhm and this Braun woman?"

"We have been unable to find out anything about Madame Braun. The relationships, real or not, are not relevant to the grave events now coming to their conclusion that will be the subject of the trial and, accordingly, we should disregard them for the purposes of deciding whether Heβ should stay in England or return to Germany."

I drafted a short report to Major Foley to this effect and was unsurprised when Heβ was transported to Germany in October 1945 and put on trial. Events after this followed an uncannily similar course to what Holmes and Heβ had forecast. Heβ lapsed into and out of lucidity in his trial, but when he declared himself fit to be cross-examined, he used the defence he had outlined to us. No one was able to lay claim to having found Hitler's body though no one seriously questioned that he was dead. Heβ was found guilty of two charges and condemned to life imprisonment, though we understood that the Soviets had pushed for a capital sentence. The Soviets, in fact, pressed for capital sentences against all those found guilty at Nuremburg and for guilty verdicts against those who were in the end found not guilty.

Although matters had largely resolved themselves, I was still intrigued by the lurid allegations made by Heβ. But nowhere was the name Eva Braun mentioned in the months after the end of the War and during the Nuremburg trials.

It was only in the spring of 1947, when Hugh Trevor-Roper published his book *The Last Days of Hitler* that her very existence and her relationship to Hitler were confirmed. My reader may imagine the frisson of excitement with which I read Trevor-Roper's book. The book also contained the astounding revelation that Hitler and Braun had married in the ruins of Berlin the day before they took their own lives. This did not of course confirm the relationships between her and Röhm, Heβ and Günsche, which were not even hinted at in Trevor-Roper's book and I can see no way of confirming them myself, as Röhm is dead, Heβ is in prison and Günsche remains in Soviet captivity. I was unable to interest Holmes in reading the book, but it did strike me that, in line with Heβ's prediction, Günsche was very anxious to make sure that Hitler's body was destroyed. At a time when the whole German state was disintegrating around him, he had arranged for Hitler's chauffeur, Kempka, to procure 180 litres of petrol – a huge amount at any time, but surely a low priority at such a time – to ensure that all trace of Hitler's body was destroyed. Why would he do this if not to render impossible any examination of the circumstances behind his death?

My reader may accuse me, even in great old age, of being an incurable seeker of the salacious, but the accusation that Heβ made to Holmes and me about the relationship between Hitler's lover and other senior members of the National Socialist circle continues to intrigue me. I cannot, however, prove or disprove it with the information I have.

Thus, and it is with a heavy heart, I pass this work incomplete to Pearson, on whom the passing of the years has also taken its toll, to add to his collection of stories which are too outrageous for publication in my lifetime.

Note by the successors of Dr Watson's literary executors:

Dr John Watson died on 28 October 1950 and the papers containing this work passed back from Pearson to Dr Watson's eldest son, Edward, who took care to ensure that they were preserved, although he does not appear to have examined them in any way.

On the death of Edward Watson in 1990, the papers were archived at the Public Record Office in Kew and lay neglected until they were passed to me, Henry Durham, late of King's College, London. I first examined them in the summer of 2015.

The reason Heβ gave for his flight to Scotland in his interview with Holmes and Watson, and the sensational allegation of a chain of sexual relationships between Braun and the trio of Röhm, Heβ and Günsche were all completely new revelations although, as any cautious scholar would swiftly point out, the testimony came from a man at the edge of reason rather than being provable facts. Holmes himself and Watson were only able to substantiate that all the people mentioned existed and that Hitler himself was not the sexless, masterful leader which he always took care to be portrayed as.

Writers on Heβ's flight just before the German invasion of the Soviet Union have all assumed that he was trying to broker a peace deal, however unconvincing that was on the evidence they adduced for this theory. None of the numerous memoirs written by the survivors from the bunker and none of the Nazi hierarchy in interrogation ever gave the least hint that there might have been any liaisons of the type described by Heβ in his interview with Holmes, or suggested that they may have been the reason for Heβ's flight.

There are two principal sources of information on the last days and hours of Hitler. The first is Hugh Trevor-Roper's book, referred to above. Trevor-Roper travelled to Berlin in the autumn of 1945 at the request of Sir Dick White of the British Secret Service and interviewed those survivors of the bunker who were in the hands of the Western Allies. His book appeared in early 1947 after the conclusion of the Nuremburg trials. It does not mention any chain of relationships between Eva Braun and other members of Hitler's circle and is more concerned in presenting a detailed picture of the figures in Hitler's inner circle – or court, as Trevor-Roper aptly called it –

than in probing the minutiae of his death. Yet where the death scenes are described, it is clear that Günsche is at the centre of the action.

The second major source is *The Hitler Book*. Otto Günsche was captured by the Soviets on 2 May 1945, transported to Moscow and interrogated relentlessly by the NKVD (the predecessor of the KGB), as they sought to establish the truth behind whether Hitler had died and how. Hitler's valet, Heinz Linge, was also taken to Moscow and interrogated. Both men were subjected to humiliating torture to force them to speak. Although *The Hitler Book* is very different in tone from Trevor-Roper's, its objectives are the same. A file, based on the interrogations, was written for the personal attention of Stalin by Fyodor Parparov and Igor Saleye. This was typed into a 429-page book and given to Stalin in its final form on 29 December 1949.

Western historians had access to the old Soviet archives from 1991, but the file given to Stalin by Parparov and Saleye had been given the designation "File 462A" with no description of its contents, and was ignored by historians. Researchers from the Institute for Contemporary History in Munich "discovered" the report that became *The Hitler Book* in 2005. The volume was first translated and widely published in German, then immediately thereafter in English.

Until 2015, no one was aware that Sherlock Holmes and Dr Watson had carried out their investigation of Rudolf Heβ in the last days of World War II, or what Heβ had said. When I read Watson's sensational recollections of his interview with Heβ, I sought to validate them in *The Hitler Book*.

The Hitler Book makes none of the suggestions made by Heβ to Holmes and Watson, but read by someone informed with the insight provided by Dr Watson's writing, it is striking how many of the incomprehensible things in Hitler's life and death start to make sense.

Röhm was executed, allegedly for his homosexuality, but this preference was not particularly unusual amongst the Storm-troopers. Watson's work is a compelling reason for thinking that the reason for the execution should be re-examined.

Then there is Hitler's reaction to the desertion of Eva Braun's brother-in-law, Hermann Fegelein, who was a leading figure in Hitler's inner circle. He sought to flee Berlin in the last week of the Battle of Berlin. *The Hitler Book* relates how Hitler was content for Fegelein to be punished by being sent to a penal battalion, but that Günsche agitated for his execution, which was then carried out. Could it be that Günsche feared that Fegelein had uncovered his secret and wanted to make sure that Fegelein was properly silenced?

Even more tellingly, the very last few scenes in Hitler's life are told exclusively from the point of view of Günsche, who is described as standing guard outside Hitler's study while Hitler shoots himself. This clearly leaves the possibility open that Günsche himself fired the fatal shot in an argument between lovers of the same woman and that Günsche then arranged for the complete destruction of Hitler's body to ensure that the true cause of death could never be found out.

There is no doubt in my mind that the revelations made by Heß to Watson have compelling evidence to substantiate them. Unfortunately, it is no longer possible to speak to any of the participants in the sombre drama of the bunker to investigate them further. The last character of those mentioned above was Otto Günsche himself, who died in 2006, and so the trail has run cold. A historian's responsibility is to tell us what happened rather than why it happened. Nevertheless, Dr Watson's memoirs may just have helped us explain the motivations behind some well-known events, which until now have been shrouded in mystery.

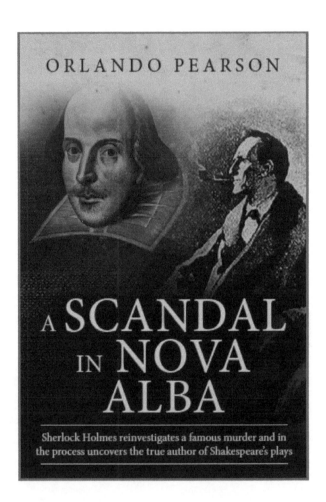

ORLANDO PEARSON

A SCANDAL
IN NOVA
ALBA

Sherlock Holmes reinvestigates a famous murder and in
the process uncovers the true author of Shakespeare's plays

A Scandal in Nova Alba

I came down to breakfast to find Holmes seated in his normal place. He did not look up from a document that had come in that morning's post. After several minutes of intense concentration, he wordlessly passed it over to me, and I took it to the window to look at it in the sunlight shining into our sitting-room. It was an undated, unsigned note written in thick black ink and the address at the top was of a hotel in Rome.

"There will call upon you tonight at a quarter to eight o'clock, a gentleman who desires to consult you upon a matter of the highest importance. Your recent services to two of the royal houses of Europe and other services rendered outwith the more elevated levels of society, have shown that you are one who may safely be trusted with matters which are of an importance which can hardly be exaggerated. Pray be in your quarters at the stated hour."

"What do you make of this letter?" Holmes asked.

"Its sender must be from the highest circles of society," I remarked thoughtfully, as I attempted to put Holmes's deductive methods into practice, "as the notepaper is of the highest quality, and the name of the hotel in Rome, Hotel di Savoia, suggests a lofty establishment".

"Good, Watson, very sound," said Holmes. "Anything

else?"

I picked up the envelope and was surprised to see the postmark was a London one from the previous day. I pointed this out to Holmes, who countered "But what does this tell us?"

"Only, I suppose, that for whatever reason, the writer wrote the note from an Italian hotel before coming to London and sending it to us from here."

"Still the same old Watson! Is it possible you fail to grasp the importance of what you have said? You observe without inferring. You state that it is written by someone from the highest circles of society, but in fact his knowledge of my assistance to two royal families suggests that the writer is himself a senior member of a royal house. Otherwise, it is unlikely he would be aware of this fact. We may therefore go further than merely to say that the writer is from the very highest circles of society. We can additionally note that the subject matter on which he wishes to consult with us is of such importance that he has not entrusted a secretary with drafting his correspondence. I deduce therefore that the member of the royal house has himself written this note in a hotel room using hotel stationery. The writer was clearly unsure of whether to send it at all, and in the end wrote it in Italy, but sent it off only once he had arrived in London. His precision over the time of our meeting combined with his hesitation in sending the note show a high level of vacillation. The English itself is of interest. It is clearly written by someone who is either a native-speaker or who speaks English at a level close to that of a native-speaker. Yet I am surprised by the use of the word 'outwith', which is used largely as a Scottish legal term meaning 'excluding'. I wonder what member of a royal family is acquainted with Scottish legal terms?"

"So what are you going to do until a quarter to eight

this evening?" I asked.

"I have a number of other commissions to perform," said Holmes breezily. "And in any case, I can do nothing useful on this case until our client arrives."

I had a number of commissions of my own to carry out and it was just before a quarter to eight on a miry evening that I arrived back at Baker Street. Precisely at the appointed time, there was a knock on our door and our client entered. He was a short, wiry man, smartly but unobtrusively dressed.

"Is one of you gentlemen Mr Sherlock Holmes?" he asked in a voice with a Celtic lilt.

"I am," said Holmes. "And this is my colleague, Dr Watson. And whom do I have the honour of addressing?"

"I am the king of Nova Alba."

"Surely, I have seen you before, Your Majesty?"

"I think not," replied our visitor. "This is the first time I have stayed in London, though I did come past your door this morning when I was getting the perfect spy of the time required to get here from my hotel."

"Ah, that must be it," said Holmes blandly, although I could see he had discomfited our visitor. "And you say you are the king of Nova Alba?"

Nova Alba! I remembered the Anglophone but Anglophobe fastness cast adrift in the north Atlantic and seemingly in a permanent state of strife. As I recalled, its present ruler and hence the man before us, had become king after a power struggle involving his predecessor, the sons of his predecessor, assorted other pretenders to the throne, and a Norwegian invader in which all but the king had either been killed or gone into exile.

"Nova Alba," said our client smoothly, "is a country which has been much misunderstood. While in the past it was a *kakocracy* of unrivalled savagery, my reign has seen the rule of law hold sway in a way it has never done before. Indeed, in many senses, it is now more liberal and at peace with itself than England is. We no longer have a censor, we guarantee free speech, and indeed some of the wilder things in life that are banned here are permitted in Nova Alba, although we make sure that those who need protecting from such things remain protected. I have been on the throne for ten difficult years, but the turbulence in my land has abated to the extent that I finally felt able to make a visit to Rome to meet the Holy Father, as I and most of my countrymen are of the Roman Catholic faith. I wanted to see him on a number of matters relating to my ascent to the throne that required clearing up. He recommended that I seek advice from you."

"Perhaps then, Your Majesty, you would like to set out the circumstances relating to your ascent to the throne on which you require clarification," said Holmes stiffly.

"My predecessor as king, as you may recall, was King Duncan," continued the king. "I was his Chief of Military Staff. I had just repelled an invasion from Norway and the king came to my palace to celebrate our victory. While he was a guest under my roof, he suffered a violent end. We found him in his bed stabbed in the side. Within a week, Duncan's sons, who as adult sons were the obvious successors to the throne, had fled. They were rumoured to be trying to muster a rebel army, but nothing more was ever heard of them. Shortly afterwards, Banquo, a fellow nobleman, and his son, also went into exile. As there was no one else of sufficient authority to ascend the throne, I was invested as the new king."

The king paused and I could see my friend becoming increasingly curious.

"So what did you wish to speak to me about?" Holmes enquired at length.

"Although I have been king for ten years, I have not as yet been crowned, and I visited the Pope in an effort to persuade him to come to Nova Alba to perform my coronation. He declined to do so as long as the finger of suspicion over King Duncan's death was levelled at me. I asked him how I might clear my name to his satisfaction, and he suggested I convene a court of Alban noblemen to try my case. If they find me innocent, he is willing to make a state visit to Nova Alba and crown me king."

There was another long pause before Holmes posed another question: "And ... did you kill King Duncan?"

"No, sir, I did not."

"And was your statement to this effect to His Holiness not sufficient to assuage his doubts?"

"I am not so much of a fool as to deny that when a man is murdered in his host's house and, as a result, the host acquires his titles, lands and fortune, suspicion against the host is a very natural reaction!" The king flushed as he spoke and I could see his reputation for a hot temper was well-founded. "I was, in fact, surprised that the Pope agreed to meet me at all, given the cloud that has hung over my name ever since the death of Duncan, and I am fully seized with a desire to satisfy him of my innocence. I would like you to investigate the killing of Duncan and to present your findings to the court."

"And does anyone else know of this plan?"

"No, sir. I have agreed the plan to engage you to investigate this case with the Pope, who suggested your name himself. Furthermore, I have told my nobles of my desire to establish my innocence, but have not intimated to them how I intend to do this. Indeed, before I went to Rome I had not formed a plan on this matter at all. I posted the letter asking to see you yesterday, after my arrival in London off the boat-train."

Holmes left another long pause before saying: "Tell me about the murder of King Duncan."

"I felt my life had reached its zenith when King Duncan came to my castle. Little did I think that this would be the prelude to the most crushing misfortune for all that this misfortune also led to my becoming king. Duncan had just bestowed the title Thane of Cawdor on me. He came the evening after our victory over the Norwegian invader, accompanied by his two sons and by Banquo and his son. After much revelling, we retired to bed at midnight. It was a tempestuous night and I felt restless so I walked around the castle to try and soothe my nerves. I encountered Banquo and his son, Fleance, on my walk. Banquo gave me this diamond ring, which he said the king wanted me to pass on to my wife." The present king drew a ring with a brilliant stone out of his pocket. "I curse the day I took this because my valet found it in my pocket the next day and people thought I had either stolen it from the king after a struggle or robbed it when we discovered his body. Banquo, Fleance and I talked for a spell and then I went back to bed. In the morning, Captain MacDuff, a hero from the battle, arrived and went into the room where Duncan lay asleep. He found a scene as if the chamber were a flesher's, with the king lying in his own blood in his bed."

So can you tell me who was in the castle on the night of the murder?"

"I have here a plan of the erstwhile castle and its grounds."

"Erstwhile?"

"Yes, erstwhile. Soon after the death of King Duncan, the Norwegians sought to take advantage of the political void created by the sudden vacancy on the throne and launched another invasion. We beat them back, but not before Dunsinane Castle and its grounds were largely ruined."

"Pray continue."

The king pointed to the plan. "The castle had ramparts, an inner courtyard and a heavily fortified central keep in which all the most senior people slept. Access to the keep was controlled by a porter. Apart from a few servants, the only people in the keep were the king, his sons Donalbain and Malcolm, Banquo and his son Fleance, and my wife and I. Everyone else associated with the estate slept in rooms built into the ramparts. Outside the ramparts were a moat crossed by a drawbridge and, leading to the drawbridge, an avenue of beech trees."

"Can you tell me who the servants were?"

"I don't take much account of them, but there was the Porter, who was a long established servant at Dunsinane and the two page boys the King travelled with, Billy Wagstaffe and Frank Flitch."

"So you are saying that unless an intruder got into the tower and escaped undetected, the killer must be from among these nine people?"

"I know or knew all of them well and they are all people I would trust. Yet what you say is true. It would indeed have been a difficult task for an outsider to penetrate the keep as the Porter guarded the only door to it and the ground-level floors were used for storage of food reserves and hence only had slits as apertures to the outside."

"You say you knew the people who slept in the central keep well. Do you not know where any of them are now?"

"My wife is no longer with us while Banquo, Fleance and the sons of the king, Donalbain and Malcolm, have all gone into exile."

"Tell me about them."

"Banquo is or was the same age as me. He was a brave

warrior and a noble soul. Fleance was about fourteen and a bright, charming lad. Donalbain and Malcolm were in their early twenties, sturdy souls though not yet bloodied in battle."

"So what is there for me to investigate? You have been on the throne for ten years while your rivals and possible perpetrators of the crime have all fled without trace or have died. Your castle and its environs – which might have afforded me some clues to the crime – no longer exist."

A proud look came into the King's eye. "For my people I need the affirmation of His Holiness and to receive his affirmation, I need to be declared innocent by my nobles, who will only be convinced of my innocence if there is a proper investigation by someone who commands respect. I have resolved I will do all that a man can do to clear my name. He who dares do more is none."

"You make yourself very clear. I will have to think about the best way to proceed. How long are you staying in London for?"

"I am at the Langham Hotel under the name of Mr Basil Scott and will not leave until I hear from you."

"Could I ask you to give me the ring that you received from Banquo as it may furnish me with some clues to this case?"

"But I have had this ring in my keeping for ten years. How can it still provide you with clues?" asked the king.

"Your Majesty is clearly aware of the small reputation I have been able to establish as an investigator," said Holmes in a voice that invited no debate. There was a pause and the king waited for him to continue, but Holmes would not be drawn any further. Eventually the king handed Holmes the ring and left our room after giving a low bow. We listened to him walk down the staircase to the front door of the house. As soon as we heard the front door open, Holmes sprang from his seat and out of the room. Within a minute he was back, nestling in his chair. I waited for Holmes to say something as I knew that he would not want any interjection from me to break his train of thought.

Finally he went to his desk and pulled out a document.

"His Majesty is clearly not the only person for whom the issue of who killed his predecessor is of concern. I did wonder whether to tax His Majesty with this accusatory document this evening, but thought I might find out more from him if I did not mention it. Do you read out to me the section I have marked in red, good Doctor."

I turned to the page directed and read:

WIFE OF THANE OF CAWDOR

Alack, I am afraid they have awaked,
And 'tis not done. The attempt and not the deed
Confounds us. Hark! I laid their daggers ready;
He could not miss 'em. Had he not resembled
My father as he slept, I had done't.
Enter THANE OF CAWDOR
My husband!

THANE OF CAWDOR

I have done the deed. Didst thou not hear a noise?

"What an extraordinary document!" I exclaimed. "Whoever wrote this is making a direct accusation of murder against the present king of Nova Alba. Where did you get this?"

"I found it rammed through the letterbox marked for my attention this morning after you had left. I have no more knowledge about it other than that it was delivered by hand and not by post, as there was no stamp or postmark on the envelope."

"So assuming the sender was also the writer, there must be somebody else intimately connected with the Nova Alba court who is here in London and who has tracked the king to our door?"

"That is so. The document is a play about the death of Duncan. It is written in a melodramatic style shot through with so many evil portents and shrieking harpies that it is rather a shame that Richard Wagner is no longer with us to write an opera on the subject, although the turbulent style and wild subject matter may perhaps suit the Italian temperament better. It covers precisely the events that the king of Nova Alba has described to us: the thane's victory over the Norwegian king, Duncan's visit to the thane's castle for the party after the battle, the thane's encounter with Banquo and his son after midnight and, finally, the discovery of Duncan's body in the morning. But, where it differs from the present king's account, is that it portrays him, in spite of manifold misgivings, as being goaded into killing Duncan by his wife, who has since passed away. It then goes on to portray further events that depart from the king's account: here Banquo is slain by agents of the king rather than escaping, and – departing from the implausible to the impossible – this version recounts the escape of Fleance, who apparently takes to the skies to flee." I would add at this point that the time that the events I describe took place was before the recent invention of powered flight by the Wright Brothers. "Whoever wrote this work," continued Holmes, "is a person of high intelligence who can predict the motives and courses of actions of the main players in a complex drama. I am not yet clear that the writer of this play is my foeman but the pursuit of him is certainly something worthy of my mettle."

"So which version of the events do you believe?"

Holmes paused and then said thoughtfully "The king is putting his throne at risk by seeking to convene a gathering of nobles to declare his innocence. Anything less than a whole-hearted endorsement of him will make his continued presence on the Nova Alban throne difficult, whereas he could simply have allowed the suspicion of guilt to hang over him and carried on regardless."

"So what motivates the person who wrote this drama accusing the king of murdering his predecessor?"

"For whatever reason, someone wants to discredit the king and it appears to be worth their while to follow him to London and trail him while he is here to do so. That is why I went out just now to see if the king was being followed as he was obviously followed here this morning when he came to check our address. Whoever followed him this morning must have been the person who pushed this manuscript through our door, but when the king left us just now he went out onto an empty street and stepped into a cab that he had left waiting outside our door when he arrived."

"So what do you make of this second person?"

"His presence in London must be unknown to the king as he had to follow the king here to find out whom he wanted to see in London – that was why I confirmed that the king had been here this morning to check the address. The king had not told anyone he was coming here; therefore, he must have been followed by someone who knew where he was staying so that that second person could post his play through our door. The latter must be an educated person to be writing in the extravagant style of the play and he must have a reason to wish the king ill."

"And what is your next move to be?"

"I must consider how I might find out more about the second person."

"Although the street is now empty, might this second person have followed the cab that brought the king here this evening, or might the cab driver have seen something?"

"I had of course thought of both those possibilities and, armed with the cab number that I took when I went downstairs, I shall speak to the cab driver tomorrow, although I doubt that I shall be able to see him before the evening."

I had a number of tasks to perform the next day and it was early evening before I returned to Baker Street. As I arrived, a cab drew up and its driver stepped out. We went up the stairs together to the quarters that Holmes and I share.

I opened the door to our lodgings and Holmes rose from his seat. The room was cold and I looked for the poker which was normally beside my chair as my war wound made it imperative that our living room had a comfortable temperature, whereas Holmes was largely impervious to heat or cold. The poker, rather to my surprise, was by Holmes's seat, even though it was obvious he had not used it to tend the fire. I asked Holmes to pass over the poker so that I could put some life into the glowing embers. Holmes appeared dissatisfied with my efforts and took the poker back. He added some further logs before using the poker and the bellows to produce a hearty blaze.

I could see that the cab-man was somewhat taken aback by all the domestic effort, but he introduced himself in a gruff East-End voice. "I'm John Turpey from Clayton Street and the Yard asked me to come here. What do you want with me? I am a poor man and could do without being called off the street."

"I wanted to ask you about the fare you brought here to Baker Street last night. There is half a sovereign here for you if you answer my questions," said Holmes in the engaging manner he could adopt so easily when he chose as he straightened himself up and hanged the poker from its hook by the fire.

"I did bring a fare here last night, sir," said the cabbie brightening up. "I was hailed by the doorman of the Langham Hotel and I brought my passenger to this street. He asked me to wait while he came in here and returned after about a quarter of an hour and we went back to the Langham Hotel."

"Anything else about the evening?"

"There was nothing special. It was quite difficult turning into Portland Place because a column of demonstrators was marching along it. Very irregular crew. Got right in the way, they did, though I couldn't hear if they were shouting out protests or anything. There's always some new model of people parading through the street, so you get used to it. I was right grateful to the doorman for picking me out among all the cabs on the street though I don't think I've ever seen a man in work so much the worse for drink. He was quite open about it too – babbling on about what the drink was doing to him, though he was so far gone and his accent so strange, I couldn't understand everything he was saying. The fare didn't say anything other than to ask to come here, though he was very generous with his tip and I was glad of the fare as business has been thin recently."

I thought Holmes would get impatient at Turpey's rambling and inconsequential description of the events, but instead he said: "You interest me exceedingly. So the doorman was in drink?"

"Yes, sir. He was hard put to open the door to my fare.

My passenger looked outraged that someone in that condition could be on the staff of such a prestigious hotel though I saw he tipped him generously as well."

"Anything else?"

"Not that I can think of, sir."

"Well, here's your half-sovereign and there's another if you can think of anything else."

When Turpey had gone, Holmes sat back and lit his pipe.

"It is strange," he said thoughtfully as the smoke swirled upwards, "to have a case that presents so many features that make identifying the criminal so easy and yet where material evidence is so lacking."

He fell silent and, after a long pause, continued.

"It's like this, Watson," he pronounced with much more of his normal mastery. "The killer of Duncan is in London. He must be one of the people who was in the central part of the present king's castle ten years ago. He knows that the Nova Alban king has been here and that he is consulting with me. But we do not know who it is or what he looks like. I was therefore very circumspect with Turpey and made sure that the poker was always in easy reach until I heard his strong London accent, which ruled the possibility out that he might have been the person who followed the king."

I waited for him to continue, but that was the end of what he had to say and he would not be drawn any further. After another hour, I retired to my room.

I was just waking up the following morning when I heard a commotion which seemed to be coming from the street. I grabbed my pistol and took the stairs two at a time as I ran down.

The front door was open and framed in the doorway was Holmes, fighting desperately with an unknown assailant, who had him in his grip. Left to themselves, it was by no means clear who would win the struggle, but I crashed the butt of my pistol down onto the head of Holmes's attacker. He gasped at my blow and let Holmes go long enough for us to bring him to the floor. I pressed the barrel of my gun to his head while Holmes twisted his arms behind his back and between us we brought him upstairs struggling all the way. It was only when fettered hand and foot with my gun pressed to his temple that he realised the futility of further resistance. Holmes's attacker was in his mid-forties, but strong and fearless.

"Who are you?" asked Holmes, but got no response.

"Are you Lord Banquo?" Holmes then asked.

A look of astonishment crossed his face.

"How do you know that?"

"I am Sherlock Holmes. It is my job to know what other men do not."

"What do you want with me?" asked Banquo at length.

"I was going to ask you the same question."

"I came here to tell you to keep you away from my son."

"Fleance?"

"I am unsurprised you know his name."

"Only because I realised you are Banquo."

"I followed Fleance here, so I know that you know him."

"Sir, I have not met your son. I know that you have a son, but I do not know where he is or what he looks like. Perhaps you would like to explain why you think I should know him."

"My son has always had a taste for irregular company which I abominate." Banquo ground out, his voice hissing through clenched teeth. His gaze wondered from Holmes to me and back. "He has been behaving very strangely over the last few days. I followed him to your door yesterday and saw him put something through the letter box. Shortly afterwards, I saw you at your door as you extracted my son's missive from the letter box and went back into your house before going out. So I know that you know my son."

"I received an anonymous document containing an incendiary play through my door yesterday. But I did not know it was from your son of whom, I repeat, I know nothing. Indeed I had no idea from whom it was. Now tell me what you know about the death of King Duncan of Nova Alba."

Again a look of astonishment crossed Banquo's face.

"How do you know about that? No one has mentioned that to me for ten years. What is your connection with this?"

"Sir, it is normally the prisoner who answers the questions."

"Very well. There is not all that much to tell. I am from Nova Alba. Ten years ago we defeated the Norwegian invaders and I visited Dunsinane castle as guest of the hero of the battle, the Thane of Cawdor, to celebrate our victory with him and his wife. I went with my son, Fleance. King Duncan did us the honour of attending with his two sons, Malcolm and Donelbain. It was a very happy evening to mark our triumph and we retired late to the central fortified part of the castle to which only we and a few select servants had access. During the night, I walked round the castle and encountered my son Fleance who was disturbed, as I was, by a violent storm that was blowing. We then crossed the path of the thane. The next morning King Duncan was found in his bed dead from a stab wound."

"And what did you do?"

"I did not know what to do. The likeliest candidates to

have carried out the crime were Cawdor and the sons of Duncan. The sons of Duncan fled straight after the crime was discovered. Fleance and I fled in a hot air balloon shortly afterwards, as I was sure that Cawdor, who had seized the throne, was going to have me arrested and put on trial. I have lived in and around London these ten years trying to keep myself afloat from money that I was able to bring here from Nova Alba."

"And why do you not mention this?" said Holmes and drew from his pocket the diamond ring that the king of Nova Alba had given us.

Banquo turned very white when he saw the ring.

"Where did you get that?" he asked in a faint voice.

"No, sir. Where did you get that?"

"I have not seen that ring since the night of Duncan's murder," said Banquo after a pause.

"And where did you get it then, I ask?" said Holmes.

"I was given it," Banquo paused. "By King Duncan."

"And why did he give you the ring?"

"The king thought that I had a taste for glittering baubles," said Banquo very quietly after another long pause. "And so he pressed it on me."

"Pressed it on you?"

"He made it very difficult for me to refuse it."

"And how did you feel about having it pressed on you?"

"I felt humiliated, sir."

"How 'humiliated'?"

"My pride was sore wounded."

"Anything else?"

Banquo ran his tongue nervously over his lips and said "As my pride was wounded, so I was proud to wound him."

"So you stabbed him?"

Banquo nodded and his breathe came out with a loud

hiss.

There was a long silence before Holmes said: "I think I see how the cards are falling. And where is Fleance now?"

"In our house is a cellar. I locked him in there before I came out."

I heard Holmes take a sharp intake of breath. When he finally spoke it was with a vehemence I had never heard before from him.

"Sir, your son's life is his own, not yours. You have no right to keep your adult son in detention. We had better get to your house as soon as possible. I shall call a cab. Watson, do you make sure that our friend makes no attempt to escape."

But Banquo was a transformed figure after his confession and was fully seized of a desire to co-operate.

"My house is near Maidenhead, Mr Holmes, and I feel the justice of what you say. My only desire was to keep my son from mixing in company that is unsuitable for a man, but I see now I cannot hold onto him forever."

"We shall go to Maidenhead," said Holmes. "And may I warn you, Lord Banquo, I will have no hesitation in summoning the authorities if you make any attempt to escape or cause a disturbance."

Banquo made no attempt to escape either from the cab to Paddington, or on the train to Maidenhead. When we arrived at his house, the door was opened by a young woman carrying a baby.

"I have remarried and have just become a father again, though we have been through a traumatic birth and my son had to be delivered with forceps," said Banquo. "I hope my new son does not share the habits of my son by my first marriage."

I expected Fleance to be banging at the cellar door. Instead, the house was silent. Banquo unlocked the door leading to the cellar and we went down the stairs to find Fleance writing at a desk. He turned as we came down the cellar stairs and looked questioningly from his father, to me, to Holmes.

"It is alright," said Holmes gently. "I know everything."

"Everything?" gasped Fleance and Banquo together.

"I know that you, Fleance, killed Duncan at Dunsinane Castle ten years ago, and I know that you only did it when the king's friendship towards you changed to lust."

"As my king was fortunate, I rejoiced in heart," said Fleance calmly in a declamatory tone. "As he was my king, I honoured and obeyed him, but as his favour turned to licentiousness, I slew him. I struck out with my ceremonial dagger when he called me to his chamber and advanced on me. My intent had been no more than to warn him off in his pursuit of unusual pleasure, but his haste to grasp me meant that my blow was a sore dunt which struck home far harder than I intended and he died in an instant. After killing him, I joined my father and gave him the diamond ring that the king had sought to give to me as a token of his favour. My father passed the diamond ring onto Cawdor when we met him walking round the castle, suggesting it should be a present for his wife."

"So why did you put the text of your play through my door?"

"For as long as I can remember, my father has told me that I would become king of Nova Alba. I had heard from my sources in Nova Alba that the present king was in Rome and that he was looking to clear his name of the suspicion of having murdered Duncan. I knew he was bound to come through London to get home and I guessed he would look to commission an independent investigator here. I went up to London and followed him off the boat-train at Victoria to the Langham Hotel, then waited outside to see where he went. I had already written my play about the murder of Duncan and had cast the Thane of Cawdor as the killer. I thought it would give any investigator something to think about and so I shadowed Cawdor's movements. When I saw him checking out the address of the leading investigator in London, it was an obvious step to implicate him by putting a copy of my play into the hands of the investigator."

"Why does your father think you will become king of Nova Alba?"

"He has long been talking about how he met some wild women after the battle against the Norwegians. They forecast the ascent of Cawdor to the throne and said that my father would be the father of future kings. I never took the prophecy seriously, but having the present king identified as the likeliest killer of Duncan seemed a good way to clear the path ahead."

Holmes turned to Banquo. "I have not had a son," he said, "but were I to have one, I would not be able to blame him for what he did when Duncan sought to misuse him. And I would not rule out behaving as you did to take the blame for a killing that he was responsible for. But I would also seek to encourage him in his pursuit of his literary interests, rather than punishing him by locking him up in the cellar. Come, Watson," said Holmes, turning to me. "Our job is only half-complete. We must return to London."

We had a first-class compartment to ourselves as we bowled back to London and Holmes elucidated on the events that had unfolded with such bewildering speed.

"It was clear from the first," he explained, "that while political advancement was the obvious motive to ascribe to the killing, it was not the only possible one. Donalbain and Malcolm, the most immediate beneficiaries of the death of Duncan, fled at the first opportunity. Cawdor seemed to me to be too hesitant a figure to carry out so heinous a crime. Ambition should be made of sterner stuff than that displayed by petty men who became willing exiles and a reluctant monarch. I considered a break-in from the outside, but the king's description of the keep of the castle showed that access to the king's sleeping quarters would have been so difficult as to rule out the possibility."

"And the servants?"

"I was inclined to dismiss the thought that they had committed a crime for political ends. Even had they done so, it was by far the most likely probability that it would have been at the behest of one of the people occupying the keep. So investigating their motives, movements and current locations did not seem worthwhile. This left the thane's wife, Banquo and Fleance as the potential killers. If it had been the wife of the thane it was unlikely to be for a political reason although it might have been for the sort of reason that Fleance did in fact kill Duncan. She, in any case, was dead, so this left Banquo or Fleance. The play I received implicated the thane and his wife, and it could only have come from Fleance once I had identified Banquo this morning. This led me to conclude that the killer probably was Fleance, however implausible an adolescent killer was. Yet a lad is capable of administering a fatal blow with a knife, so Fleance's youth did not rule him out."

"But Banquo confessed! What made you think that his confession was false?"

"A good detective should always test out alternative hypotheses. I had no real evidence against anyone so the only way I was going to find the killer was through surprising a confession from him, but I always knew that I would have to test the confession's plausibility. So when Banquo confessed, I had to ask myself some questions. Why was Duncan travelling with two page boys rather than his wife? How likely was it that he would make advances to a burly courtier who could obviously defend himself, as opposed to a youth whose silence could more readily be relied upon? How likely was a man of Banquo's type to be impressed by a ring with a glistening stone and how much more likely was a callow youth with a head for poetry to be impressed by it? I had therefore at least to test the hypothesis that Banquo's confession was covering for someone and the person for whom he was covering could only be his son. When Banquo said that he had locked his son into the cellar, the opportunity to tax Fleance with the killing was too good to miss. You saw how readily he confessed to the stabbing when the true motive was put to him."

"So what are you going to do now?"

"I will have to talk to the present king. I assume that he will want to continue with the process he has started although he may be reluctant for the full story behind Duncan's death to come out. Once one identifies one case of this type at such a senior level in society, one is never sure how many further cases may be left to uncover, or indeed how to investigate them."

Events in Nova Alba do not generally receive comprehensive coverage in the London press, but readers may recall certain subsequent incidents even though, at the time, they may not have seemed to have had a common causation.

When Homes discussed the matter with him, the king of Nova Alba did not want the true reason for the stabbing of Duncan to come out. Nevertheless, Holmes armed him with sufficiently powerful arguments and reasoning for the trial established under the aegis of Alban noblemen to return a verdict of "Not proven". A "Not guilty" verdict was withheld in the absence of a clear identification of the actual killer. This verdict was sufficient to persuade the Pope to make a fleeting visit to Nova Alba on his way to a state visit in Scandinavia and to play a minor role in the coronation. Cawdor stayed on the throne for another twenty years after his visit to London and was replaced as king by Lulach, Banquo's younger son who, after his difficult birth, had grown to be a strapping lad. As a special gift to mark the accession to the Nova Alba throne of Banquo's younger son, who had been resident for so many years in the area, Maidenhead Borough Council sent a gift of saplings from the famous Burnham Beeches up to Dunsinane to replace the avenue that had been destroyed in the second Norwegian invasion.

And London theatre-goers will remember the long succession of fine dramas which Fleance wrote, using as nom de plume the name of one of the Dunsinane Castle page boys, Billy Wagstaffe. This pseudonym caused considerable confusion in literary circles, with some critics inclined to ascribe the pieces to the other page boy, Frank Flitch, instead.

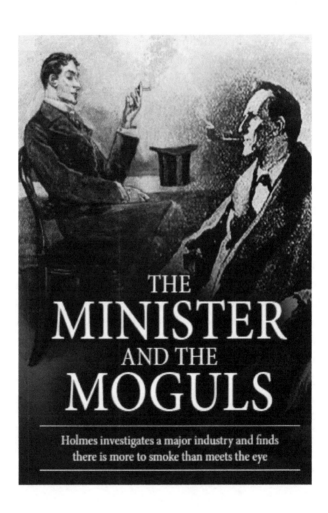

THE
MINISTER
AND THE
MOGULS

Holmes investigates a major industry and finds
there is more to smoke than meets the eye

The Minister and the Moguls

It is with reluctance that I narrate the events that follow. In all the other stories I have told, I have been able to explain, even in the rare cases where the narrative did not conclude with the apprehension of the criminal, what happened and why it happened. While the events of this story are relatively clear, and while the final result delivered was that sought by the person who petitioned Holmes for his help, I did not understand then and do not understand now, how this was achieved, or even if the result achieved was the consequence of Holmes's work. I am likewise at a loss to explain some of the actions that Holmes and others took following the resolution of this drama, and the extent to which they are the result of the events I describe. Holmes was always adamant in refusing to discuss this case with me and, when he heard that I was committing it to my records, asked me to delay publication of it until after the death of us both. Thus, even if some sharp-eyed reader is able to identify the solution to what remains to me an unsolved mystery, I would advise herewith that there is no point in seeking me out to explain it to me.

I had returned to our lodgings from my club, where I had been spending a lot of time. This was because Holmes had been largely absent from Baker Street for some weeks and had not involved me in any of his recent cases, if indeed there had been any.

When I opened the door to our living room, Sherlock Holmes was sitting with a man who subsequently became a household name in one of the two main political parties. He held a relatively lowly Cabinet position at the time of this story. Afterwards, he left government altogether for a period while remaining a backbench Member of Parliament, but returned to a Cabinet role later, and eventually attained the high office for which he was being already widely tipped even at this early stage of his political career. His true identity I shall withhold, just as I will withhold both the year and even the decade of the events which this narrative relates.

"Ah, Watson!" called out Holmes as soon as I had entered the room. "You could not have come back at a better time! Mr Lawler is engaged in outlining a problem which promises to be both unusual and of the greatest interest."

I was not a little shocked to find our humble lodgings hosting Mr Lawler, but I took my seat and waited to hear what he had to say. At Holmes's request he started to explain his problem from the beginning.

"Our government is in the process of drawing up its budget for the next financial year," said Mr Lawler smoothly, as he lit a cigarette. "It will be delivered to the House in two weeks from today. Drawing up a budget is normally a question of so plucking the goose as to obtain the largest amount of feathers with the least possible amount of hissing, but this year we have a pressing requirement to increase our revenues so as to meet some particular government needs. The Royal Navy, the principal reason for this country's lofty international power, is in urgent need of strengthening and we are looking to raise extra money next year to do this. One of the government's principal sources of revenue is from the taxation of tobacco, but we seem to have reached a limit on the amount we can extract from this source. Our tobacco retail prices are the highest in Europe. We cannot therefore obtain more money by forcing up the retail price of tobacco further, as all that will happen is that demand for home-sourced tobacco would decline, with the shortfall met by increased smuggling of lower-priced product sourced from overseas."

"Could you not impose a special levy on the tobacco companies' profits so as to raise the tax you need without raising the retail price?" I asked.

"We have already had some discussions with the tobacco companies on that idea and they have said that they will add any levy on their profits onto the retail price as they will need to maintain their level of profitability in this country. They have also launched some of their products with the same brand names and packaging in overseas markets where lower excise taxes mean they command a much lower retail price, although it is also fair to say that the companies obtain lower margins. This price differential makes it easy for smugglers to bring them over here and sell them at a profit. This also means that the government does not get any of the excise duty that would arise on a regular sale. A levy would merely accelerate the amount of smuggling and so the gain to the government from the levy would be offset by a decline in the tax take from a lower volume of products sold."

I could tell that Holmes was starting to feel impatient. He stood up and began to pace the room with smoke trailing from the cigar he was holding. Finally he turned to Mr Lawler and said "My dear Mr Lawler! I am not clear what you want me to do. On the one hand you want to raise more money from the tobacco companies. On the other hand you say the obvious routes to achieve this are blocked. I fail to see what purpose this discussion is serving."

"There are only three major tobacco companies in this country: Commonwealth Tobacco, Thompson's and International Tobacco. Between them they control over ninety-eight per cent of the market and the first two of them have over eighty per cent. We want you to find evidence of anti-competitive behaviour by these companies. If we can demonstrate market collusion between them, then we can impose a one-off fine, and the bad publicity it would generate would make them most reluctant to pass the fine on in the form of higher tobacco retail prices. And so we can invest in our fleet to make this country great."

"You would like me to find hard evidence of market collusion? Surely, Mr Lawler, you have armies of sharp-pencilled civil servants who can generate evidence of any such practices?"

"The people to whom you refer are excellent at generating data and extrapolating trends, Mr Holmes. It is like those protesters who worry about the recent spate of cold winters. They confidently state that it is caused by the slow pace of industrialisation which is failing to offset the cyclical growth of the polar ice-caps. From this they predict that if trends continue as at present, we will in fifty years time once again have frost fairs on the Thames." Mr Lawler laughed at this improbable prognosis and lit another cigarette before continuing. "But they are unable to predict what the weather will be like next week. And so it is with our data analysts: If you wish to know what the annual volume of tobacco to be sold in the country will be in a couple of decades' time, they can give you an excellent and well-reasoned response. But ask them how much is being consumed now and how much is purchased through irregular outlets, then they are a good deal less confident. What we need is something more tangible. Something that I can use to bring the tobacco companies to heel."

Holmes looked very doubtful. "Mr Lawler," he said. "I am already engaged by your government on a separate project which you may or may not know about, but of which I cannot mention the nature in case you have not. I accordingly do not have the resources at my disposal to undertake an investigation of the kind you are suggesting. What I can suggest is that my friend Dr Watson here does some initial research on my behalf but under my supervision, and it may be that by the time he has completed this, I will be free to become more closely involved."

The Minister and I were both taken aback by this suggestion – I, because I had no expertise at all in the area proposed, and the Minister because this solution, which is such a regular feature of the collaboration between Holmes and myself, had evidently not occurred to him.

"I have always taken a great deal of interest in Dr Watson's writings," said Mr Lawler warmly. "And he is always most assiduous at performing investigations at your behest, Mr Holmes. I am sure that, properly instructed by you, he will be more than capable of undertaking at least the initial stages of the required research. And, should such a thing tempt either or both of you, I am equally sure that the government could make a positive outcome in this commission worth your while either in terms of financial reward or honours."

Holmes paused before responding and then he asked "And for on-going expenses?"

To my astonishment, Lawler plunged his hand deep

into his pocket and pulled out a bundle of grubby-looking notes secured by a red rubber band. "We recognise that you will incur expenses before you can come up with any findings. Here are £1,000 for immediate outgoings and you may revert to me personally at my Ministry for any further advances you need to cover costs you may incur."

Holmes wrote out a receipt for Mr Lawler and I waited until the latter had gone before making any comment.

"Why do you think I can research something like this when a department full of Mr Lawler's staff are unable to do so?"

"My dear Watson! This is an interesting commission, but one for which I have no time at present. You, on the other hand, shuttle listlessly between your club and here. You have, if I may say so, looked a little out of sorts lately, and I am sure an investigation, undertaken with expenses to be recovered at a princely rate, will benefit you."

I had expected Holmes to proceed to brief me on how I should carry out the necessary research, but instead he rose from his chair and disappeared out of the door.

I was at something of a loss as to what to do, but, as so often in my collaboration with Holmes, I decided to do what he asked regardless of the difficulties with which the task presented me. I reflected how I might research something as large and complex as the tobacco industry and drew heavily on a cigarette as I did so. I had been for many years a customer of Bradley's of Oxford Street, of whose own brand of cigarettes I was a steadfast devotee. I liked the idea that in a world increasingly being taken over by machine-made cigarettes, he still had his own proprietary brand. I looked at the ornate packaging and read the legend "These finest cigarettes, containing select tobacco blends, and once made and packed by hand on our own premises here in Oxford Street, guarantee highest smoking pleasure." I had consumed many thousands of Bradley's cigarettes over the years and had read the legend on the pack many times. But I had never before noticed the word 'once' in the description of the cigarette manufacturing process on the packaging. I had been under the impression that Bradley's cigarettes were still made by hand on the premises. I had got to the end of my cigarette and drew on another before I decided that Mr Bradley, whom I knew well by sight, might be a good person with whom to start my researches, especially as his shop lay not far from the route to the London Library in St James's Square, where I determined also to consult with my friend Lomax, the sub-librarian.

When I got to Bradley's, the proprietor greeted me in a friendly manner as I asked for a packet of his cigarettes.

"So are your cigarettes still made on site?" I asked and pointed out the insertion of the word 'once' in the legend on the packaging.

"Oh no, sir, not for several years. When we first put a legend on our packs, it was because we knew we would soon stop manufacturing by hand so it read 'These finest cigarettes, containing select tobacco blends and made by hand on our premises in Oxford Street, guarantee highest smoking pleasure.' It was then much easier to insert the word 'once' when we switched from making our products ourselves by hand to buying them from one of the big manufacturers without drawing attention to the change in the process." Mr Bradley's face creased into a conspiratorial smile and he was unable to restrain himself from breaking into a low-pitched chuckle at the success of his minor deceit.

"So what happened to the ladies who used to make your cigarettes?"

"Well, in the end, sir, we only had one. Carmen, she

was called. Very beautiful girl with a lovely voice. She's become a professional singer. Very talented chanteuse she is."

"So why did you make the change?" I interjected as I was anxious to avoid Mr Bradley expatiating about Carmen.

"Well sir, cigarette machines can make two hundred cigarettes in packs a minute. Dear Carmen was good, but couldn't roll more than six cigarettes a minute so the cost advantage is obvious."

"So these are no longer your proprietary product?" I asked.

"I own the brand name, sir, but I buy the actual cigarettes from Commonwealth Tobacco who have factories across the country."

"And the rest of your assortment?"

"They are all bought from the big manufacturers. There's Commonwealth Tobacco, Thompson's and International Tobacco."

"And are there no small, competing manufacturers?"

"Oh no, sir!" Mr Bradley chuckled again, seemingly amused by my ignorance. "Since mechanisation of manufacture, those three have bought all the others out. The big three sometimes keep the names of the old, small companies on the pack, but that's a bit like me referring to the cigarettes of Bradley's of Oxford Street as having been made on the premises. There are in fact only three companies of any significance."

"And how are your dealings with them?" I asked.

"They're very efficient businesses, sir. They always deliver when we place an order and a salesman calls from each one almost every month. They bring in new versions of their products – look at this menthol-flavoured variant of Smooth Purple. The manufacturers of Georgiov introduced something similar last month. Or packs which make special price offers like this pack of Clayton and Bertram which is offered at 2d off. I expect that International Tobacco, the manufacturers of Dollar, will do something similar soon as well."

"Fascinating," I said, trying to adopt the easy manner that Holmes could adopt so well when trying to persuade people to give him sensitive information. "And what part of your shop's takings come from tobacco?"

"Well, we don't really look at it like that, sir. For us, tobacco brings people into the shop and they buy tobacco, on which we make a small margin, and then buy other goods, on which we make more. Tobacco is very good like that because it does not take much space."

"So if you don't mind how much you make on tobacco, how much do the suppliers make?"

"I'm sure I couldn't say, sir. Most of the cost of a packet of cigarettes is made up of tax and excise duties and I'm only the final link in the chain of supply to the customer. When there is a budget, the suppliers put through a price increase to reflect any tax increases. I expect there will be another shortly after the Chancellor delivers his next budget. And they each put through an additional price increase of their own at about the same time each year."

"Don't you resist their price increases?"

"Oh no, sir! We'd go out of stock if we did that and that would help no one but my competitor down the street. There are lots of tobacconists but very few tobacco manufacturers, so there is no negotiation. We simply pass the increase on to the people who come into the shop to buy tobacco. They grumble a bit, but in the end they get used to the higher price. You know yourself how you occasionally cut down on tobacco but always go back to it."

I thought of how prevalent tobacco smoking had been even at school and how I had been a regular consumer of tobacco ever since, irrespective of its price and the state of my own finances.

"So you are selling a product where the price does not really change the demand for it?"

"Up to a point, sir. We have noticed an increase in people coming in trying to sell us product sourced from overseas where taxes are lower and they can buy it cheaper retail than we can get it from the supplier. There's obviously a demand for what they are trying to sell, but it's illegal for us to sell it, and we wouldn't touch it, though others would. The more prices go up here, the more smuggled stuff is going to come through."

"How does tobacco get smuggled?" I asked.

"People coming through the ports bring it in. You may have heard it described as bootleg product. That's because some people bring it in the leg of their boot. But you can only bring a limited amount in like that. The big players use all manner of devices to bring it in – either dropping it off on beaches for collection or putting it into containers carrying other goods. I've even heard of it being smuggled in hidden in specially modified coffins ..."

Mr Bradley's voice trailed away as though in awe of the smugglers' ingenuity. I felt I had learnt as much as I could from Mr Bradley, so I continued on my way to the London Library.

Crossing Piccadilly, I noticed a hawker selling antimacassars from an impromptu market stall. As I watched, a gust of wind blew up a flap on the canvas and I noticed a large stack of packets of Holmes' favourite cigarette, Gold Bush, beneath. I stopped at the stall and asked for a pack. To my surprise, the hawker at first denied he had any cigarettes to sell. However, at my insistence, he grudgingly passed me over a pack for which he wanted a price about a third lower than that which I would have been charged at Mr Bradley's shop. When I looked at the pack, it was the same as the UK pack except that all the text on it was in Spanish.

"So where did you get these?" I enquired blandly.

"I only man the stall," said the hawker, looking anxiously round. "But the gentleman behind you may be able to help you."

I turned and all but collided with a swarthy mountain of a man who was standing right behind me.

"What do you want to know about my products?" snarled the giant in a voice which did not suggest that he was anxious to offer information.

I decided there was no purpose in asking any questions and walked on. When I glanced back I could see the ogre engaged in a furious and one-sided altercation with the hawker.

It was a relief to get to St James's Square. Lomax was more than willing to help me, though he did warn: "We can look up what there is in the published material, Dr Watson, but there won't be much. All the companies try and reveal as little about themselves as possible and this sort of thing isn't really our speciality." He wrinkled his forehead a little and then said "But, I remember there was something in the newspapers about them last week."

He retrieved a copy of *The Times* from the archives and we read about two delegations, each led by one of the leaders of the two biggest tobacco companies, Commonwealth Tobacco and Thompson's, to the Chancellor of the Exchequer, asking him to moderate the tax increases on tobacco in the next budget. The article identified the leader of Commonwealth Tobacco as John Vincent Harden while Thompson's Chief Executive

Officer was James Grace. We looked them up in Who's Who and found the following entries:

John Vincent Harden: Chief Executive Officer of Commonwealth Tobacco, market-leading Anglo-German tobacco company, and non-executive director of several companies; patron of Covent Garden Opera House and the Aachen Opera Festival; owner of 200,000 acres of land in Shropshire with houses in London and Paris; married to Elizabeth, daughter of Lord Sorrell.

James Grace: Chief Executive Officer of Thompson's Tobacco, global tobacco company; owner of the Syrret Racing Stables with Derby winners in 1898 and 1899; member of Chorley Club; married to Gwendoline, daughter of Mr and Mrs Bryant of Mayfair.

Compared to what I had learnt from Mr Bradley, it was a thin harvest that I had reaped at the London library, but Lomax assured me that there was little more that could be found out about either Harden or Grace from publicly available sources. As is my wont whenever I am at the London Library, I borrowed a couple of volumes from the shelves before I returned to Baker Street to find Holmes slumped in his armchair, deep in thought. He perked up when he saw me.

"So, Watson," he asked brightly. "What have you found out?"

I started talking to Holmes about what Mr Bradley had told me. I told him about the elimination of small tobacco companies, and the resultant small number of players supplying Mr Bradley's shop, and how they all passed on price increases to the tobacconists, which got passed on to the consumer. "The three big players control the entire market," I concluded. "Surely there must be something wrong with that?"

I waited for a modicum of praise from Holmes, but instead he replied "Well, it is, I suppose, fair to point out that you trained to be an army surgeon and not a businessman. What you have described is what happens in all industries once there is effective mechanisation. The more successful players buy out the small ones. The few players that are left can then use their power to sustain a high level of pricing in the market and to keep competitors out. You will find the same pattern with suppliers of soap and beer. In the end you finish up with three or four companies. The most efficient market of all is politics, where the number of parties selling ideas is a mere two of any significance although other parties do make an impact from time to time. There is nothing illegal in what you have described, though it does mean that the consumers suffer at the expense of the tobacco manufacturers' shareholders as price competition is reduced. Did you manage to establish anything which was not in any case self-evident before you started your investigation?"

I had been rather proud of what I had found out in my interview with Mr Bradley, especially as the hawker had confirmed some of it straightaway, and was downcast by how dismissive Holmes was about it. I then read out to him what I had extracted from Who's Who about the chief executives of Commonwealth Tobacco and Thompson's. To my surprise, Holmes reacted much more positively to this.

"If we are to find out anything useful about anti-competitive practices in the tobacco companies," he said, "it must be personal things. It is perfectly legal for companies in the same industry to follow the same strategy. It is if they communicate with each other on the strategy that they are vulnerable to legal challenge. I am not sure, from the descriptions of Harden and Grace, whether I should send you to watch opera or horse racing."

And with that he pulled out his own files of information. They contained some rather more personal observations about the tobacco moguls. He started with John Harden and his file stated "Agitating for a peerage. Will not get one while still a Chief Executive." Of James Grace, his files stated "Gambler for big stakes and has a poker face. Wealthy so he can afford big risks." To my surprise, he had not only entries against the Chief Executive Officers themselves, but also against their wives and their wives' parents. About Elizabeth Harden he read that she organised charitable works in her home town of Guildford and that she was a former opera singer. Of Gwendoline Grace he read "Married to James Grace. Consumptive so spends time at spa towns – Buxton, Bath, Evian, Aix-la-Chapelle, Vichy."

"Well, Watson," he commented and looked me up and down. "There is at least money in this case if nothing else. Mr Lawler has been most munificent in the sum he has so irregularly provided to meet immediate outgoings. How would you like to go spend some of it in an agreeable city that used to be the capital of the Holy Roman Empire? The Aachen Opera Festival starts next week and John Harden is bound to be there. It is a shame Mr Lawler cannot lend you his opera hat that he had with him when he visited us. You can re-acquaint yourself with the voices of the de Reszkes who are singing there and whom I always associate with our great Devon triumph."

"You want me to go to Aachen to listen to opera?"

"Please go and enjoy the opera, but your true mission is to find out what you can about John Vincent Harden. He must be a well-known figure in the town. Find out where he lives, what he does, where he goes, whom he meets. And keep me informed of your progress."

In less than a day, I had got the boat-train to Dover, the ship to Calais and the Vienna Express which passed through Brussels before I alighted at Aachen. The town was abuzz with the festival and I experienced considerable difficulty in finding a room. In the end I was able to locate quarters only in the most prestigious hotel in the town, Preußischer Hof. After resting for a while from the rigours of my journey, I wandered round the town centre and soon came to the opera house. Holmes's regular use of German quotations in our conversations had compelled me to brush up the German I had learnt at school, and I was able to understand the local papers with their previews of the opera to be heard. Nevertheless, I was relieved that the man who served me at the box office was a local polyglot, who told me he had been working at the festival for many years and was himself a true opera enthusiast. I got into conversation with him as I bought a ticket for the following night's performance of Mozart's *Così fan tutte*.

"You have an excellent seat, sir, even though it is one of our last ones," he told me, after he had served another customer. "People often don't like sitting in the slips of the dress circle, but in this theatre you can see the whole stage even from the side." He broke off again as another customer came in before continuing. "The singing – I've heard the rehearsals – is going to be first-class and it will be the same all week. Perhaps you would be interested in a ticket for *Fidelio* which starts on Monday?"

"How are sales going?" I asked, anxious to keep him talking.

"We are well on the way to being sold out for every performance. People come from far and near to the festival and we're all looking forward to the first night tomorrow.

Your seat in the slips will enable you to observe the whole auditorium so you will see how full we are."

"Do people come from overseas, as well?"

"Well, we are close to France, the Netherlands and Belgium here – that's why speaking several languages is useful in this job – so we get people coming from there too."

"And do all the town's leading citizens come as well?"

"Oh yes, sir. The mayor or Bürgermeister and most of the leading citizens will be present as well as all the festival sponsors."

"Oh really?" I said, doing my best to appear casual. "And who may they be?"

"The biggest sponsor is Commonwealth Tobacco. They have a factory near here and are much the largest employer in town. Their leader, John Harden, is an opera lover and comes here every night entertaining guests."

"Commonwealth Tobacco is a slightly strange name for a tobacco company in Germany," I commented.

"Indeed, sir. Until a couple of years ago, the sponsor was a local tobacco company – a family firm called Bruckmann. You may have heard of the German *Mittelstand* – the vast number of small family companies, which are such a feature of German business life compared to the large industrial combinations you have in the United Kingdom? Nevertheless, although these family companies are generally very solid and stable, every family has its price. My understanding is that Commonwealth Tobacco were happy to pay the top price to acquire Bruckmann. In the end, a large company is almost by definition more successful than a smaller one, and the big ones swallow the small ones. I think this is more usual in the Anglo-Saxon world, but it applies here as well."

I thought I was about to receive the same basic lessons

in economics that I had had successively from Mr Lawler, Mr Bradley and Holmes himself, so I hastily turned the conversation back to John Harden.

"Is Mr Harden often in Aachen?"

"Mr Harden, as far as I am aware, and I admit that we are not discussing my special area of expertise, divides his time between London and here, but he has always come to the opera festival and sits in the middle of the front row of the dress circle every night surrounded by his guests. From your seat in the slips you will be able to see him with his wife for *Così fan tutte* tomorrow."

I felt I had learnt as much as I could about Mr Harden for the moment and resolved to go to *Fidelio* as well.

"Your decision you will not regret, sir!" exclaimed the helpful opera enthusiast as he handed me my ticket.

I found a post office and telegraphed my intentions to Holmes. I then went to a cafe on the Hauptstraße for something to eat and when I came back there was an answer for me. He told me to watch out for any audience participation from Mrs Harden. Holmes's responses are often sphinx-like in their obscurity and I had no intention of letting this one disturb my enjoyment of the opera.

The next day I visited the Cathedral. The construction of this magnificent edifice was started by Charlemagne. I reflected how the power of economics was starting to subvert national boundaries and circumscribe the ability of national political leaders to act. Charlemagne would not have had to engage in spying on his subjects in order to extract money from them. Absolute power is much easier to exercise and is perhaps less corrupting than the exercise of limited power. My musings at the Cathedral and wandering round the Old Town, made my day pass very swiftly and in the evening I betook myself to the opera house to hear *Così fan tutte*.

The house was as full as my friend at the box-office had said and, as I waited for the overture to start, I cast my eye around the audience. The man at the centre of the front row of the dress circle, surrounded by dinner-jacket-clad gentlemen and ladies in evening wear had to be Mr Harden. He was engaged in animated conversation with two gentlemen to his left and the one seat that was empty was the one to Mr Harden's right. As I watched, I saw a lady in dark evening wear, which contrasted with the extreme pallor of her skin, make her way past the other spectators to take her place next to Mr Harden. The evening passed in a whirl of the most glorious music. I left my seat promptly at the end and decided to wait at the front to see Mr and Mrs Harden leave, but though I waited for a long time, they did not come by. So I returned to my hotel, where I passed a peaceful night.

The next day I went to the Post Office and telegraphed Holmes about the events of the previous evening. I had also formulated the plan of buying one of the new Eastman cameras to see if I could make a so-called 'snapshot' of Mr Harden, his wife and those surrounding him. I mentioned this too in my telegram to Holmes. As I left the Post Office, I bumped into my friend from the Box Office who wished me a pleasent evening at the theatre in his charming accent. I dropped again into the cafe on the Hauptstraβe and enjoyed some of the fine local cakes and then went to a specialist camera shop to buy the camera. I took detailed instructions on how to take a 'snapshot' and then headed back to the Post Office, again crossing the path of the man from the Box Office, to see if there was a reply to my telegram. Holmes had written: "Now you have seen what all the ladies do, be true and do the same on Monday. Then return to London." Most of this seemed like a code but the last part was at least clear.

I went to *Fidelio* on Monday night and once again watched as, rather irregularly, Mrs Harden took her place after Mr Harden had arrived. She sat next to him, the whiteness of her skin emphasised by his black jacket, and I raised my camera to my eye and took my 'snapshot'. The button clicked.

With a sigh of relief I sat back in my seat to wait for the lights to go down. Suddenly I felt a tap on my shoulder and I turned to face two imposing theatre ushers. One said something in German which I did not understand. As I was explaining that I did not speak much German, my neighbour said "They are requesting that you come with them."

We went out of the auditorium and into a little lobby, which was deserted. One of the ushers seized my camera and said in accented English "I will take your camera to the Box Office where you may collect it at the end of the performance." The other usher looked on, but when his colleague had my camera with its precious photograph in his grasp, he went off to continue his business. I was anxious not to let my camera out of my sight so I chased after the usher who had seized my camera, protesting vigourously. Suddenly a familiar voice said.

"Follow me, Watson! I am here to make sure the man from the Box Office does not get hold of this. I think we have drawn quite enough attention to ourselves already."

We exited through a side door and went back to my hotel. Once in my room, Holmes leant back in the arm-chair and drew deeply on a cigar before he spoke.

"I think it is only fair to you, Watson, to explain what I have been investigating," began Holmes. "A few weeks ago, I was approached by a government minister – not Mr Lawler – who wanted me to investigate the toxic effects of tobacco. He wanted someone who was an experienced chemist, fully independent of other researchers and a tireless investigator. We are all aware of the positive effects of tobacco – for general health as a purgative, for the mind as an aid to concentration, and for the senses, as a source of pleasure. Tobacco is a natural leaf-based product and so its consumption ought to be an innocent enjoyment. The government is concerned that the tobacco companies are adding ingredients to increase the desire to smoke to a level higher than would be natural for the product and that may have an adverse effect on health. It has charged me with carrying out the research."

"And what would the consequences be if you found anything of that kind?" I asked, lighting up a cigar of my own.

"A manufacturer is of course allowed to add what it wishes to its products to increase their desirability but not if the additive has a deleterious effect on the consumer. If this were the case, then the additional ingredients would need to be eliminated."

"And what are your findings so far?"

"Nicotine in tobacco has of course been known about for a long time. It was first isolated from the plant as far back as the eighteen-twenties. It is a stimulant to the nervous system and this explains the agreeable effect that tobacco inhalation has on the smoker and why the urge to consume a second cigarette or other smoking product after having consumed one is so strong." Holmes briefly closed his eyes and drew deeply on the cigar he had lit up, so that its tip glowed, before he continued. "I was quite struck by what you said about the addition of different flavours to the tobacco which you described to me from your visit to Bradley's. Mr Bradley mentioned menthol as being one of a variety of new flavours being tried, and recent introductions have included vanilla and cherry. My research, my notes on which are in this file here, has shown that menthol enhances the enjoyment of nicotine to such an extent that the smoker's desire for an additional cigarette is increased exponentially. Indeed, as your sottish friend, Isa Whitney, discovered in the case of laudanum, to the extent that further consumption becomes impossible to resist."

"But, Holmes! You have just said that a manufacturer is allowed to put anything he likes into his product as long as it is not toxic."

"There is, is there not, something slightly disconcerting about a widely available product with a legal additive which produces an unnatural craving for it? And the manufacturers must know about this. Otherwise the main two, Commonwealth Tobacco and Thompson's, would not be introducing two new products with the same new additive at the same time. But the fact that it is 'slightly disconcerting' is not a sufficient reason for withdrawing an additive that is legal, though I pointed out the effect menthol has to the officials in the Ministry of Health when I made my initial submissions."

"And what is the relationship between your chemical investigation and what I am investigating?"

"That is something I was very tempted to ask Mr Lawler himself when he visited us. The ministers in charge of public health and those charged with managing this country's finances both seem to be more than usually interested in the activities of the tobacco companies and yet seem unaware of each other's activities. I carried out the first engagement under representations of the strictest secrecy, however, so I could not disclose to Mr Lawler the nature of my investigation. It is only after much thought that I am disclosing it to you." Holmes again raised his cigar to his lips. "How marvellous a thing is a cigar!" he exclaimed. "Tobacco rolled in a tobacco leaf and nothing added to it." He paused and again closed his eyes reverentially as the smoke rose from the end of his cigar before he said: "And now we must investigate what you have found!" and with that he disappeared into the bathroom with my camera.

"Excellent, Watson!" he exclaimed, when he emerged. "This is just what we were looking for! We will go back to London tomorrow!" And without saying any more, he tucked the photograph he had developed into the impressive-looking file of data in which he had gathered his researches into tobacco additives.

We arrived back at Victoria Station early in the morning of the Wednesday. Holmes had said nothing further to me about the case on the journey home. Instead, his sole topic of conversation was Mozart's librettist, Lorenzo da Ponte, and the wonder of his operatic plots – *Così fan tutte*, *Don Giovanni* and *The Marriage of Figaro* – all shot through with scheming and subtlety yet with da Ponte remaining in full charge of the story's direction. Rather than going back to Baker Street, Holmes insisted we make straight for Tobacco House, headquarters of Thompson's. My friend presented his card at the reception and, even though we were asking to speak to the Chief Executive, it had its customary commanding effect. Within five minutes we were sitting in front of Mr James Grace. Holmes put his file of data on the table in front of him as he sat down opposite.

"Mr Holmes, your name is obviously known to me through the writings of your friend Dr Watson. What can I help you with today?"

"I have been commissioned by the government with finding evidence of market collusion between the major tobacco companies in the United Kingdom."

"Mr Holmes. The tobacco companies are well aware of their responsibilities. We do not talk to each other about pricing or strategy."

"It is noticeable, is it not, that prices go up at the same time by the same amount and that product innovations tend to be copied by the different companies?"

"What you describe, Mr Holmes," said Mr Grace, with barely suppressed impatience, "is a well-ordered market. The three companies adopt their strategies independently and do not talk to each other. I am powerless to influence what my competitors do just as they are powerless to influence us."

"It is possible, is it not, for companies to talk to each other without talking to each other?"

"I fail to follow you, Mr Holmes."

"When an employee leaves, he tends to go to another tobacco company."

"We try to discourage that. Our senior employees have six-month cooling-off periods – the maximum that is allowed under restraint of trade laws – to prevent precisely that."

"Even so, your strategy of raising prices and introducing new variants of your products has hardly changed, so when one employee leaves and goes to another tobacco company, knowledge of your plans goes with him."

"There is absolutely nothing illegal about what we have done."

"What about your previous Chief Scientific Officer?"

"He left us six months ago."

"What is he doing now?"

"I understand he is now working for International Tobacco."

"Why did he leave you?"

"Mr Holmes, your inquisitiveness may not have any

limits, but my willingness to answer your questions does."

"What can you tell me about mentholated products?"

"Menthol is a legal additive that we struggled to add to our product in a way which was acceptable to the public. Since you obviously have at least half an idea of the way our business works, I may as well tell you that this was why our previous Chief Scientific Officer left us. It had been his task to develop a mentholated product and this he failed to do. His replacement, whom we were able to attract from Commonwealth Tobacco, was able to achieve what we wanted in a short space of time and we have now introduced a mentholated product to the market albeit later than our main competitor. After the cooling-off period stipulated in his contract, our last Chief Scientific Officer went to work for the number three player on the market, International Tobacco. Long may he fail to achieve there what he failed to achieve here!"

"What do you know about menthol's influence on the propensity to smoke?"

"Mr Holmes! You have asked me enough questions. All that we do here and indeed all that our competitors do, as far as I am aware, is entirely legal. We comply with all government regulations, pay more taxes than any other industry, and provide employment to thousands of people across the land. I must ask you and your friend to leave and bid you a good day."

Holmes stood up to leave and as he did so, he carelessly let the photograph I had taken in Aachen fall out of the file. He made to snatch it up from Mr Grace's desk, but Mr Grace got to it first. He picked it up, looked at it briefly, and handed it back to Holmes. "I request that you leave or I will call the Company's security guards."

We were soon back in Baker Street. Holmes sat silently in his chair. "We were warm, as the children say," he mused, but would not be drawn on further steps. I sat all evening awaiting a further comment but none was forthcoming. In the end I left him to his ponderings and went to bed.

Early next morning I got up and noticed our cigarette stocks were running low and went down to Oxford Street to replenish. In Bradley's shop I picked up a newspaper. This carried on its front page a report on a swingeing fine imposed on the tobacco companies. Commonwealth Tobacco and Thompson's had agreed, without any admission of wrong-doing, to pay substantial fines for anti-competitive practices.

Mr Bradley was in a conversational mood.

"Pleased to see you, sir!" he said, and at my bidding got me five packs of his proprietary product. As a favour to Holmes, I also got several packets of Gold Bush.

"So what do you make of this fine for the tobacco companies?" I asked.

"Well, it seems to happen all the time to the big businesses – banks and the like," observed Mr Bradley sagely. "They're always being fined for some irregularity or other. I presume they are too good at avoiding normal tax so the government is reduced to forcing one-off payments out of them. Well, there's no danger of my little shop ever being big enough for that to happen to me!"

There seemed no answer to that, so out of curiosity I asked "And how are the menthol products selling?"

"Strange you should mention it, sir," he said. "Commonwealth Tobacco and Thompson's have both said that the introduction has not delivered the sales they were hoping for and are withdrawing all stocks. This is very unusual as we've had no lack of interest for them in our shop. I am even thinking of getting a mentholated version made of our own product if my manufacturer will supply me."

The paper carried two further announcements:

Mr Lawler had surrendered his junior Cabinet post and, although remaining a Member of Parliament, was going to work as a non-executive director at International Tobacco. It was stressed that Mr Lawler's focus would be exclusively on International Tobacco's overseas business and thus that there was no impropriety in his stepping into the role directly from a position in the British cabinet.

And John Harden was retiring from his post as Chief Executive Officer of Commonwealth Tobacco. He had been nominated for a peerage and was going to act as the government's adviser on business ethics. The paper commented that as Chief Executive Officer of a global organisation, he could not have been expected to know about allegedly anti-competitive practices in just one country for which his company had been fined. Accordingly the offences, of which his company continued to maintain its innocence, were no bar to his elevation to the House of Lords or to his being honoured with the advisory postion he had been given.

I hurried back to Baker Street. As I arrived at the front door, a cab drew up and Mr Lawler stepped out. We went up the stairs together and went into the sitting room where Holmes was at the dining table awaiting breakfast.

"Mr Holmes," said Mr Lawler airily. "I am happy to say that both Commonwealth Tobacco and Thompson's have agreed, after long negotiations and without any admission of wrong-doing, to pay substantial fines for anti-competitive practices. The sums we have secured in fines will be sufficient to build the additional ships required for the Royal Navy. It is indeed fortunate that we have been able to resolve this matter without you needing to become involved. I would be grateful if you would return the

£1,000 I gave you to defray your costs, subject of course, to the deduction of any amounts you have had to disburse during the course of your initial investigations."

I had had no chance to brief Holmes on the stories in the newspaper and I could see that he was at a temporary loss for words at the sudden termination of the commission.

He came to however and, looking slightly dazed, put on the table the receipt book, his receipts of expenditure and the still largely intact bundle of notes. I reached for my own receipts, but Mr Lawler raised his hand, picked up the bundle, looked at it hard from sideways on, signed the receipt book and tucked the cash into a capacious pocket. He then put two creased ten pound notes onto the table, thanked us briefly for our efforts, bowed, and closed the door behind him. I did not hear him descend the stairs but after a few seconds, I opened the door leading out of our flat and saw that he was gone.

I told Holmes what I had read in the newspaper. He listened wordlessly and then crumpled up the receipt that Lawler had signed and hurled it into the middle of the grate, where it was soon consumed by the flames. To my surprise, he then took his dossier on tobacco additives and consigned it to the fire. It took a while to ignite before it flared up, crackled briefly and disappeared in smoke up the chimney. A transformation came over him and he switched from the energised, self-possessed individual I normally portray in these stories into a wordless, listless presence. He left his breakfast untasted and, for the only time during our friendship, he chain-smoked, lighting each cigarette with the still smouldering stub of the previous one. His head hung low as if he felt some abiding sense of shame. His breathing became laboured and irregular, his eyes sank into his head and his brow took on the beetling appearance I associated with a return to his drug-fuelled habits from which I had had to work so hard to wean him.

I had been unable to follow the course of events and I felt reluctant to ask Holmes about a situation in which, despite what Mr Lawler had told us, he clearly felt he had failed. We sat in silence. I passed the time leafing through the newspapers and when interest in these failed me, my attention switched to the programme from the performance of *Così fan tutte*, which I had brought back with me. This had notes in both German and French, but not in English. It was therefore quite time-consuming to read, as to understand the text I had to switch between the two languages to find the version that I could follow best. I had just got to the end of reading an account of the performance history of the opera when I noted that, where the German referred to the first performance in Aachen as being in 1802, the French referred to an 1802 performance in Aix-la-Chappelle. The name sounded familiar. Then I remembered that this was one of the spa towns that Gwendoline Grace had been described in Holmes's notes as attending. I decided to return the books I had borrowed to the London Library and to raise this connundrum with Mr Lomax. He had, as usual, a ready explanation: "Aachen markets itself as a spa town under the name Aix-la Chappelle, Dr Watson. Most people seeking to take the waters want to go to France, so rebranding was the town's strategy to lure them to Germany. Aachen is a spa town at least as ancient as the French towns, and has the hottest waters in Europe."

Every time I investigated something about this case, it seemed to throw up some new sleight of hand: the shifting of employees between the different companies, the misleading description of the manufacturing process on Mr Bradley's proprietory cigarettes and the use of Aachen's French name to promote itself as a spa town.

Had the pale figure in the theatre really been Mr Harden's wife, or had it been the consumptive Mrs Grace? And what, if anything, did these things have to do with the decision of the two biggest tobacco companies to pay substantial fines for anti-competitive behaviour, the withdrawal of mentholated cigarettes, Mr Lawler's appointment to International Tobacco, or the elevation of Mr Harden to the peerage? Was there a connection between all or any of these events, or were all these changes part of a process that predated our investigation? I had no way of knowing and, when I returned to Baker Street, I realised I had no way of finding out as Holmes remained slumped where I had left him and gave no response to any of my questions.

I stayed up with him until the clock on the local church tower chimed three o'clock in the morning. Then, unusually, it was he who fell asleep prone in his chair before I turned out the lights and retired to my room.

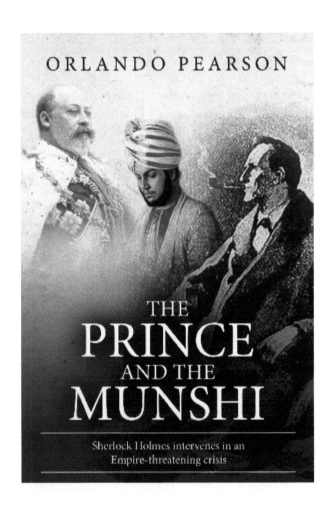

ORLANDO PEARSON

THE
PRINCE
AND THE
MUNSHI

Sherlock Holmes intervenes in an
Empire-threatening crisis

The Prince and the Munshi

"Somebody must be taking a wholly disproportionate interest in us," murmured Holmes in his blandest tone one morning, "as they are making a highly professional job of abducting us." We had taken a walk before breakfast to buy cigarettes and newspapers. At the junction of Baker Street and the Marylebone Road we found ourselves boxed in by three carriages with covered windows. Seized by twelve masked men in dark, forbidding clothing, we were forced inside. Against such odds and particularly once pistols were pressed to our temples, any effort at resistance would have been pointless. And so it was that we found ourselves rattling through London's streets with our hands and feet fettered.

My friend had an extraordinary knowledge of London streets and he whispered to me where we were going: "Baker Street ... left into the Marylebone Road ... on into the Euston Road ... south down Gower Street ... Bloomsbury Street ... into St Martin's Lane ... left into William IV Street, Agar Street, into Chandos Place and – inevitably – into Maiden Lane. Well, they didn't make that very difficult."

Dark shrouds were put over our heads and pistols pressed anew to our temples as we were dragged out of the carriage, across a pavement, into a building, up a flight of stairs and bundled into what appeared to be a small larder as there was a strong smell of food. We heard the twist of a key in the lock. In spite of the cuffs that bound my hands and legs, I was able to remove the shroud from my head and tried to make some sense of where I was in the darkness.

"We are in Rules, Watson," said Holmes casually. "This is the oldest restaurant in London. It was established by Thomas Rule in 1798 and has remained a favourite locale for the most prominent members of society ever since."

At that moment the door was unlocked and a masked face looked in.

"Perhaps we might have some breakfast?" Holmes asked the mask benignly.

There was a guffaw and we heard the masked face call "They want us to bring them breakfast!" to another of our guardians, who also burst out laughing.

The door was closed and then almost immediately re-opened as we were dragged into a large dining room.

It is my custom in my narratives to protect the identity of the many illustrious personalities whom I have, in my own small way, been able to serve as part of my work with Holmes. In many cases I have also modified some of the events I saw. In this instance, however, my story would be without meaning if I did not disclose the true identities of all the personalities involved, or forbore to give an accurate description of the events that ensued, even though this will make publication of this story impossible for many years to come.

To read more of this adventure go online at:
www.OrlandoPearson.com

Further Works by Orlando Pearson

ORLANDO PEARSON

THE TRIAL OF JOSEPH CARR

In this masterly re-imagining of Kafka, Sherlock Holmes discovers who is persecuting Joseph Carr and why

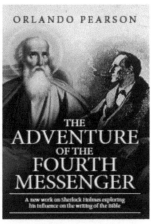

ORLANDO PEARSON

THE ADVENTURE OF THE FOURTH MESSENGER

A new work on Sherlock Holmes exploring his influence on the writing of the Bible

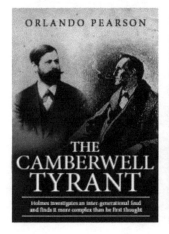

ORLANDO PEARSON

THE CAMBERWELL TYRANT

Holmes investigates an inter-generational feud and finds it more complex than he first thought

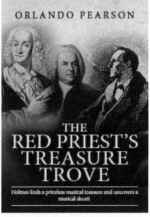

ORLANDO PEARSON

THE RED PRIEST'S TREASURE TROVE

Holmes finds a priceless musical treasure and uncovers a musical deceit

About the Author

Orlando Pearson commutes into the City during the day and communes with the spirit of Sherlock Homes by night.

He is at his happiest when applying the techniques of the great Baker Street detective to everyday problems such as how to get a seat on a crowded train or which queue of several to join in order to get the fastest service.

He lives with a wife and two children near the location of Wisteria Lodge.

More information at: www.orlandopearson.com

Lightning Source UK Ltd.
Milton Keynes UK
UKHW021030210420
362023UK00006B/82